GHOSTS

CURSED MANUSCRIPTS
BOOK 6

IAIN ROB WRIGHT

ULCERATED PRESS

WITH THANKS TO MY PATRONS...

Julian White, Emma Neil, Blanche Auxier, Wendy Daniel, Jan Willard, Fear kitty, James Cradock, Valena Smith, Renee, Lola Wayne, Sarah C, Wendy Daniel, Lisa Vaughan, Belinda Murray, Simon Longman, Lanie Evans, John Claunch, Lorraine Wilson, Fiona Thompson, Luis Roco, Terry Watson, Clark Kent, Candy, Lindsay Carter, Steve N, Rach Kinsella Chippendale, Maxons, Chris Jones, Jonathan & Tonia Cornell, Chris Hicks, Sandra Behrens, Carl Donze, Chris Nelson, Rigby Jackson, Linda Paisley, Karen Roethle, Carmen Hammond, Russell Wilson, Michael Pearse, Mark Ayre, Virginia Milway, Suzie Roush, Katrice Tuck, Adrian Shotbolt, keepsmiling, Minnis Hendricks, Kelli Herrera, Phil Brady, Steve Haessler, Darrion Mika, Karen Lewis, Suzy Tadlock, Kaarin Chadwick, mari meisel, Jayne Smith, Susanne Stohr, CJMac, Stacey, Amanda Shaw, Connie France, Gillian Moon, Robin, Stephanie Everett, Linda Heafield, Ali Black, Elizabeth Thompson, Stainedglasslee, Stacey, guitarmangrg, Diane Rushton, Stephen Moss, Jean Geill, Elizabeth Auclair, Adrianne Yang, Linda, Leslie

Clutton, Sarah Chambers, Kat Miller, Sara Boe, Carole, Nigel Crabtree, Becky Wright, Claire Taylor, Caryn Larsen, Leigh Hickey, Steve Griffith, Diesta Kaiser, Fiona Thompson, Mark Horey, Gian Spadone, Mark Stone, Rachel Stinnett, Billie Wichkan, Deborah Shelton, Pauline Stout, Angelica Maria, Katie Potter, Jordan Rasmussen, Deirdre Lydon, Bobbie Kelley, Vicky Salter, Melissa Potter, Debbi Sansom, Stewart Cuthbertson, Nicole Reid, Bruce W, Clark, carrieanne, Mark Harvey, Mark Simpson, Graeme McMechan, Jacqueline Coleman, Vanda Luty, Ruth F Phelps, Donna Twells, Katie Warburton, Susan Kay, Nick Brooks, Stewart Barnes, Nigel Jopson, Gemma Ve, Steven Barnett, Sally Jayne Dainton, Tania Buss, Lee Ballard, Emma Bailey, Clive, Robert Smith, Oscar Booker Jr, Trevor Oakley, Leona Overton, Susan Hayden, Jennifer Holston, Kelee S, Terence Smith, Michelle Chaney, Roy Oswald, Paul Weaver, Linda Robinson, Chris Aitchison, Michael Rider, Deborah Knapp, Bread, Beth Thurman, Cass Griffiths, Debbie Ivory, David Lennox, William Matthews, Kim Slater, Hazel Smith, Laurie Cook, Margaret McAloon, Paul, Neil Grey, Catherine H, Sherrie, Brian McGowan, Pam Felten, Carol Wicklund, Mary Meisel, Deborah, Lady Aliehs, Rachel Mayfield, Kerry Hocking, Maniel Le, Andre Jenkin, Lawrence Clamons, Gary Groves, Mike Prankard, Dan Garay, Rona Trout, Mark Pearson, Mary Kiefel, Emma, Karen lewis, Eddie Garcia, Tracy Putland, Laura Monaghan, Boy Stio, Emily Haynes, Pam Brown, Sharon Campbell, Scott Menzies, Deirdre Gamill-Hock, Allison Valentine, Marika Borger, Joe Wardle, William Cahill, Kristin Scearce, Lisa McGlade, Jay Evans, Janet Wilde, Mark Junk, Sarah Atherton, Phil Hope, Trudy Bryan, Joanne

Wheatley, John may, Stacie Jaye, Kirsty Mills, Louise, Kenneth Mcintire, Adam Thayer, Jonathan Emmerson, Susan Rowden, Becki Sinks, Becki Battersby, Derek Titus, Phil, Rebecca Strouse, Stacie Denise, Sarah Powell, Paula Bruce, Stella, Sandra Lewis, Windi LaBounta, Stephanie Hardy, Janet Carter, Lisa Kruse, Gillian Adams, Lauren, Clare Lanes, Jacqueline Scifres, John Best, Stacey Arkless, Nate Stephenson

QUOTES

"Social Media made y'all way too comfortable with disrespecting people and not getting punched in the face for it."
   - Mike Tyson

"I am scared of ghosts. I know they don't exist, but I still am."
   - Mimi Chakraborty

"Friends don't let friends make TikTok's alone."
   - Anonymous

THE START...

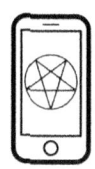

"Oh my God, your hair is on fleek, girl!"

Stef flicked her bleached blonde locks over her shoulder and struck a hip-jutting pose. "I know, right? It's like a whole thing. I'm so fuckable right now."

Hannah cackled. "I would so turn gay for you."

"Control yourself, babes!"

Hannah apologised and went over to the vanity table opposite Stef's double bed. She still wondered if her bestie had discovered the wet patch she and Dan Salter left last Saturday night during the house party, but she hadn't said anything. Hannah had been so drunk she had nearly let him stick it in her butt. Fortunately, her backside cherry remained intact – a gift for her future rich husband. One day, all of her hanging around outside Villa Park would bag her a footballer for sure. If not, then she would go on *Love Island* and make a fortune for herself as one half of a power couple.

"You got your phone set up?" Stef asked as she pouted

in front of the full-length mirror beside her bedroom door. "We gotta get on this, girl, before it goes stale."

"I know, I know. I'm just setting up the camera." Hannah's iPhone had a retractable tripod glued to the case, so she splayed the plastic legs and tilted the phone, ensuring its multiple lenses pointed at the centre of the room. Then she selected the Clip Switch app and set a twenty-second timer. "Okay, we're counting down. Let's get in position."

Stef pranced away from the mirror and joined Hannah on the fluffy pink floor rug running parallel to her bed. Both of them were barefoot, their French manicures only a day old. Hannah wore tight jeans and a shimmery green blouse, but Stef was going all out with a slinky blue dress that made her boobs look amazing. Hannah might have worn something similar if she had any of her own to speak of.

I'm so jel. Every bloke goes straight for her just because her figure is better than mine. Lucky bitch.

There's still time, Hannah's mum always said, *you've only just turned sixteen*. But it was getting harder and harder to believe.

The Clip Switch app beeped the beginning of a countdown.

Hannah and Stef stood in front of the camera. Stef grabbed a piece of A4 paper they'd stained with used tea bags to make it look old – just like something Jesus would've read from during one of his talks. On it, they'd written the words from a video they'd watched online. A video that was rapidly being imitated and duetted by anyone who was anyone.

With almost two million followers, Hannah and Stef

had a duty to jump on new trends as soon as possible. They were leaders, not followers. Influencers, not sheep. Stef&HanStuff was earning them almost five hundred quid a week into the shared bank account Stef's mum had helped them set up, and the channel was still growing. Soon they would be richer than their parents. Stef already planned to move out – to get away from her embarrassing wino of a mum and have boys over to her own place whenever she wanted – but Hannah got along well with her parents. She didn't want to leave home. Instead, she would buy a massive house for them all to live in. One with a swimming pool and a Jacuzzi.

Her iPhone gave a long beep and started recording via the app.

Hannah tossed back her curly brown hair and struck a pose.

Stef jumped right into character, flipping a sideways V-sign at the camera and pouting her glossy pink lips. "Hey my sexy friends, how ya doing? It's Stef here."

"And Han here."

"And we're about to... summon the dead."

Hannah had been smiling, but now she put her hands against her cheeks and silently screamed. The new trend was supposed to have a spooky vibe, although some influencers went completely overboard with Halloween decorations and fake blood. Stef and Hannah didn't need to go that far, mainly because they had Stef's big boobs and two pairs of pretty feet. It was messed up how many more views they got on videos where they were barefoot. Most of their followers were probably gross old men.

But as long as the money keeps coming in, where's the harm?

Stef usually wore glasses, but never on camera, so she had to squint for a moment to get her eyes adjusted to the words on the page. Then she started to read them out loud.

"*Con nomi segreti e porte nascoste, riporta i miei perduti e falli conoscere. Revia soul nocto. Revia soul nocto. Revia soul nocto. Amen.*"

Hannah let out a bloodcurdling scream, clutching at her throat. She choked and gagged, thrashed and panicked.

Stef's expression fell. The sheet of stained paper fell from her hand and floated to the fluffy pink rug. "H-Hannah? What's wrong with you? Stop it!" She grabbed her friend by the arms and yelled in her face. "The power of Christ compels you! The power of Christ compels you!"

They both erupted in laughter.

The story surrounding the incantation was that it could summon the dead. The words were ancient, put on the Internet by an evil witch. If you said them out loud, an angry spirit would appear behind you and slit your throat.

It was a load of rubbish, of course, but it was a laugh.

Stef doubled over in fits of giggles. Hannah was cackling too, but mostly because she was chuffed by her own performance. Her acting skills were unreal. Her viewers were probably clutching their chests after the fright she'd just given them. Maybe she and Stef should have had Dan hide in a closet and jump out to slit their necks with a fake knife. That would've been lit. Maybe they could do it in a follow-up video.

Hannah beamed into her iPhone's triple lenses while

Stef continued laughing hysterically. "Don't forget to tag us in your own videos and share our channel. This is Han." She looked to her left, waiting for Stef to do her sign-off. "This is Han!"

Stef remained doubled over, still cackling away. Or maybe not cackling at all. In fact, was she…?

"Stef, are you okay?"

Stef grunted and waved a hand at Hannah in a panic. Not knowing what to do, Hannah just stood there as Stef collapsed to her knees and started raking her fake nails down the outside of her throat, which was now bulging in a totally minging way. It looked like she'd swallowed an apple. Two apples!

Stef turned her head to look at Hannah.

Shitting hell!

Her eyes were bulging in their sockets. She tried to speak, but her throat was all blocked up. Drool spilled from her mouth, and instead of words, something disgusting fell from her lips.

Beetles.

A fuck-tonne of beetles.

"Stef, gross!"

The fat, shiny bugs streamed from Stef's mouth in a violent black eruption that covered the fluffy pink rug completely. Oily brown stains spread out on the carpet, making everything glisten.

Hannah backed off, colliding with the full-length mirror by the door and cracking the glass with her butt. Her legs became stiff, and she knew if she tried to use them, she would topple over.

She was having a panic attack.

The bugs continued piling on top of each other on the rug, clumping together and forming a writhing black mass that grew and grew and grew.

Stef moaned, her eyes bulging more and more and more…

…until they popped right out of her skull and dangled on her cheeks. More bugs spilled out of the sticky red sockets. Her body collapsed onto its side, creatures spilling from every orifice.

Hannah screamed so loudly that her voice echoed inside her own skull like an alarm bell. She vomited inside her mouth and it dribbled down her chin. The only thing she'd eaten was a rice cracker that morning, but she tasted it again right now.

The bugs clumped together, rising, rising… forming shapes… creating limbs.

Arms and legs.

Slowly, a human shape emerged from the writhing, chitinous mass and took a step towards Hannah. She cowered in front of the cracked mirror, unable to move anything except her trembling arms, which she threw out in front of herself pathetically as a shield. Her left hand was bleeding from the broken glass, glistening red blood dripping from her fingertips.

She tried again to scream, but the air had already escaped her lungs. All she could do was glance at her still-recording iPhone and wonder how many of her followers were watching this. Two million people, and not one who could help her.

What is happening? What did we do?

Hannah spoke her last words as the creature slithered towards her in a frantic mumble. "W-we didn't know it was real. We didn't know!"

CHAPTER ONE

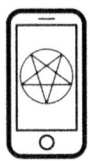

Shane punched his olive-green Toyota Land Cruiser's scuffed-up steering wheel and sounded the horn three times. Evie immediately appeared on the front doorstep of her house, while her mother Sarah – Shane's sister – stood behind her, glaring down the driveway. Sarah's shoulder-length brown hair was tied up in a messy bun, and she had on her nurse's scrubs, clearly ready to go to work. Shane waved a hand apologetically but avoided catching her eye.

Evie shouldered her backpack and hurried towards the car, yanking open the passenger door and letting in the cold February air. "You're late again, Uncle Shane."

"Get in and close the door," he said, grabbing an empty crisp packet from the passenger seat and tossing it into the back. "The heaters are on the blink."

Evie tutted. She slid into the worn leather passenger seat and slammed the door closed, then immediately shuddered, her gold-painted fingernails retreating into the sleeves of her maroon school blazer. "Shit, you weren't kidding. It's fucking freezing in here."

"Hey, watch your language. Does your mum know you talk like that?"

She drilled him with a stare, her large green eyes identical to her mum and Shane's – the family emeralds. "What do you think?"

Shane chuckled. He was no fan of authority, so how could he judge? "Okay, buckle up."

"You're late again," she said for the second time.

"I know, I know. I'll talk to your teacher."

"Don't you dare. I'm not twelve. I'll just have to take the flak for it. Again."

He struggled to put the Land Cruiser in gear but eventually managed to pull away. Sarah still stood on the doorstep, so he beeped his horn again to annoy her. He hadn't intended to be late.

Shit happens. Not my fault society likes to place so many restrictions on itself. Time is a human construct, and entirely meaningless if you stop adhering to it.

Evie was pulling a face and looking into the back of the car, which Shane liked to use as a portable skip.

"What's wrong?" he asked her.

"Will you please get a new car. It's so embarrassing when my friends see me in this. How is this piece of shit still running?"

"It's a warrior. There's nothing this car can't handle. I bought her from new and she's taken care of me ever since."

"Bought her new when?"

He shrugged. "Two-thousand-eight, I think."

She shook her head and pulled her iPhone out of her blazer pocket, muttering to herself as she unlocked it.

"How's your mum?" Shane asked, not wanting to lose her attention this early into the journey.

"Huh? Oh, she's good."

"Care to elaborate?"

"Nope."

"Great! Well, I'm good, too, if you wanted to know."

Without looking at him, she said, "You don't look it. You look like crap."

"Jeez, Evie. What side of the bed did you get out of this morning?" He pulled down the visor mirror and gave himself a quick once-over. His wavy brown hair was an odd shape due to how he'd slept, and it was long overdue a cut. His face was, admittedly, a little flush. "Okay, maybe I could use a comb and some aspirin, but you don't always have to be so brutally honest."

Evie pulled her gaze away from her phone and turned to him. Unlike her mother, her hair was copper-coloured. Shane had been banned from calling her 'ginge' after making her cry at her sixth birthday party. "You made me promise when I was a kid," she said, "that I would always tell you the truth. It was our little pact, remember?"

He remembered it well. When Evie had turned twelve – she was fifteen now – he had caught her smoking in an underpass near her house. Instead of going ballistic and telling her mum, he had made her a promise, that he would always be on her side so long as she was honest with him. That was his duty as a cool uncle, right? To be the keeper of secrets and a steadfast ally. The person Evie could turn to with a drug problem or unwanted pregnancy.

To pick up after my flailing sister whenever she fails at being a single parent.

"I've had a few late nights," Shane admitted with a shrug. "Not much to do after work other than drink, eat, and masturbate."

Evie groaned, but she smiled at the same time. "You're so gross, Uncle Shane. Maybe if you got yourself a girlfriend you'd actually have a life. Forty-year-old men don't do well on their own. They start to decay."

"Thirty-nine. Your mum said that, didn't she?"

"Uh-huh. I think she worries about you."

"Or just likes to criticise my every move."

"Nah. She's like that with everyone."

Evie went back to her phone, flicking a finger up and down the screen. This was the way most of their interactions went lately. Sometimes, he would make an unwise attempt at talking about music or films, but that never went well. She still didn't believe him that Reel Big Fish was an actual real-life band.

"What are you watching?" he asked when he noticed she was watching a video.

"Just some stuff on Clip Switch."

He groaned. "That's the app where people do stupid viral dances, right? The one that caused a bunch of dumb Florida kids to eat dishwasher tablets? You know it's run by the Chinese government, don't you?"

She gave him a derisory grunt. "You should write about that in your magazine. The weirdos and conspiracy nuts will love it."

"Hey!" He might have argued with her, but she was right: most *Splatt!* readers were indeed weirdos. *Most of the writers too.* Playfully, he gave her a dig on her forearm. "Cheeky sod."

She immediately winced and pulled away. "Ouch!"

"Whoa, sorry." He pulled his hand back and held it up defensively. "Didn't mean to hurt you. Are you okay?"

She rubbed at her forearm gingerly. "Yeah, it's okay. I accidentally cut myself during woodwork at school. It's still healing."

"Oh, okay. Be careful, huh?"

She nodded.

He pulled off the highway and headed for Evie's school. While it wasn't private, it was highly respected as being the best state school in the area. Its catchment didn't extend to the nearby town of Redlake, where Evie lived, but luckily, back when she'd first enrolled, he'd still had enough connections left to pull some strings. It was one of the few times his sister had been grateful for his existence. They might have had their differences, but they both wanted what was best for Evie.

He flicked on his indicator and took a right turn. "You know, the world is pretty interesting when you pay attention to it, Evie."

She looked up at him with a gormless expression. "Huh?"

"That phone shows you the world through a filter. Nothing you see is real. Just... look up every now and then to remind yourself that you're still awake, okay?"

"Awake?"

"Yes, awake. They want to keep you sleepwalking because it makes things easier for them."

"Easier for who?"

He shook his head and sighed. Where to begin? "I'm talking about the people in power. They want us all staring at our screens twenty-four-seven to distract us from paying attention to their greed and treachery."

"You mean the government?"

He snorted. "The government is just a front for those who are really running things. Look, all I'm saying is that you should challenge everything you see. Never stop asking questions, all right? Anything coming at you through a screen is usually designed to distract you."

"You sound a little crazy, Uncle Shane."

He smiled at her, glad to see she had at least listened to him. "Sometimes the truth is crazy, darling niece. It'll be your job to fix things one day – your generation – so work hard at school and be ready."

"Yeah," she said with a smirk. "I'll try to be on time every day, for starters."

He grumbled. Kid was too smart for her own good.

"Ooh!" She leant forward and twiddled with a knob on the dashboard. He was still rocking a tape deck, but the radio worked well, which Evie demonstrated by jacking up the volume. "God, I love him," she said dreamily. "I'm going to track him down one day and force him to marry me."

Shane frowned, finding the racket unfamiliar. "Who?"

"Harry Styles! Do you live under a rock? I'm obsessed with him. He's so fit, it's not even funny."

"I'll take your word for it." He reached over and lowered the volume to a respectable level.

Evie went to turn it back up again, but her phone chirped and distracted her before she could follow through on her defiance. She glanced at her screen, but this time her brow furrowed and her lips turned downwards.

"Everything okay?" Shane asked.

"What? Oh, um, yeah, fine." She turned the phone around so the screen was face down against her knee. "Just one of my mates asking where I am."

It was plausible enough, but her manner had definitely changed. The message had bothered her. Maybe, if he knew how to deal with teenaged girls a little better, he would inquire further, but it would probably only make her clam up on him if he tried. Cool uncles didn't pry.

They reached the school road, which was chock-a-block with cars despite the bell having already rung. It always annoyed him how there were a mere dozen parking spaces for a hundred frustrated parents. It started everyone's day off the wrong way. No one wanted to play grumpy dodgems right after breakfast.

Shane pulled up outside the main gate, blocking part of the road. A Citroën beeped its horn behind him, but he ignored it until the driver had no choice but to inch slowly around his passenger side. Shane felt the stranger's glare as they passed.

"Thanks for the lift," Evie told him sarcastically as she climbed out of the car. Her worries seemed to have disappeared now, and she was back to her petulant self.

"No problem," he said. "Hey, wait a sec."

She turned and ducked her head back inside the car. "I'm already late, Uncle Shane."

"So what difference will another minute make? Just... make the most of these days, okay? It only gets worse from here on out."

"Gee, thanks. What an inspirational start to my day."

"Yeah, that kinda sucked, didn't it? Okay, well, how

about this? It's not how many times you get knocked down, it's how many times you get back up. And never eat yellow snow."

She raised a russet eyebrow at him and exhaled. "I suppose that'll have to do. Enjoy your day, Uncle Shane."

"You too, Evie."

She slammed the door and hurried through the gate. A smattering of other tardy kids made Shane feel less guilty, but not enough to dispel the vague sense of shame washing over him.

I really should get my shit together one of these days.
Nah.

He took his foot off the brake and stamped on the accelerator, pulling out in front of a white van that had been about to pass him and causing the driver to punch their horn. Now that he no longer had a teenaged passenger, he could finally drive properly. By the time he exited the slip road back onto the highway, he was already doing eighty.

Shane made it to *Splatt!*'s office on the edge of Redlake's tiny commercial district twelve minutes later. He toyed with grabbing a McMuffin from the McDonald's drive-thru across the road, but decided it might be a little too rebellious, seeing as he was already forty minutes late for work.

Parking his Land Cruiser next to Bernard's ruby-red Alfa Romeo Brera, he got out and entered the empty reception area at the front of the building. They had let Naomi go three months ago now, so there was nobody at the desk, only a notice telling visitors to pick up the phone in order to reach someone upstairs. Shane entered the stairwell and started up, yawning all the way.

Splatt! Magazine lived mostly on the building's first floor, spread out across a few offices, a conference room, and an open-plan working area. The ground floor was full of old digital printers and packing machines, but those operations had been transferred to the magazine's parent company years ago, so they were all covered in dust now. It was an old building. The windows too small and the fibreboard ceilings too low, but it was a home of sorts – a place Shane had spent the last ten years of his life after leaving his previous, short-lived career as a mainstream journalist.

God help me.

When he entered the open-plan area nicknamed "the floor", there was no one around. Flatscreen monitors occupied a half-dozen empty desks, all displaying screensavers. Only one room in the office was big enough for everyone to gather in, so Shane headed for the conference room.

As soon as he opened the door, all eyes turned on him, prompting him to give a two-handed wave. "Morning."

Bernard, standing at the front of the room with a finger pressed against a projector screen, glared at him from behind his spectacles. "Ah, Shane, punctual as ever. We were just going through the dire financial performance of the magazine. Nothing for you to worry about."

Shane grinned sheepishly and placed himself at the back of the room next to Rachel, *Splatt!*'s pretty young intern. She would be next to go if the layoffs continued, but seeing as she'd only recently turned twenty-four and still lived with her parents, she would be more than okay. The rest of the team, though, would be on the scrapheap. "My cat broke down," he said. "Couldn't be helped. Had to call a vet."

Rachel chuckled, her little nose wrinkling. She had on a blue shirt over a white vest, along with jeans and desert boots. It was a very masculine outfit, but somehow she was still entirely feminine. Her eyes lit up when she smiled. Standing next to her made Shane feel old.

Bernard let out a sigh and continued with whatever he'd been saying. Graphs filled the screen in bold, ominous colours. None of it looked hopeful, but Shane didn't concern himself with any of that. His job was to write articles about the weird and the wonderful – and that's what he did. He did it so well, in fact, that if the magazine went bust, he would in no way hold himself responsible. Print magazine was just dying out, simple as that. As with most things, the Internet was to blame.

Fuck the web. Except for porn and illegal movie downloads. And Wikipedia. Wikipedia makes my job so much easier.

Also Ozzy Man.

The meeting went on for another thirty minutes, lacking even the merest sliver of positivity. In a shit-stained nutshell, fresh out a squirrel's backside, the magazine's subscriptions were on a downward spiral and newsagents were reducing their shelf space for printed media. *Splatt!*'s only growth area was its website, but they had been recklessly slow in getting it off the ground. It was probably too late now.

Plans for the upcoming quarter included hiring a web and marketing expert and increasing advertising spend on social media – a strategy that would either save them or bankrupt them. More likely the latter. They had reached a fork in the road. The only other option was to give up and go home.

Shane exited the conference room ten minutes later and went over to the coffee machine. Craig came and joined him, a fellow caffeine addict. He was the magazine's other lead columnist, and a healthy competition existed between them – if competition involved Shane being a much better journalist in almost every regard.

"Hey, Shane," he said, marching on the spot to make up his steps for the day. The whole office knew about his mission to lose two stone. "Oof! You look like shit, mate."

"Will people stop telling me that? I had a bad night's sleep, that's all. I'm fine."

Craig didn't look so great either, even at five years younger than Shane, so he thought he should really keep his comments to himself. At least Shane had been handsome for the first half of his thirties and all of his twenties. Craig had a bent nose and Dumbo ears, as well as perpetually bad breath. Also, he could do with losing four stone.

Better keep those steps up.

"Sorry, buddy," he said, still marching nowhere. "I just thought you might be feeling rough or something. You got anything in the chamber this week?"

Shane finished pouring his coffee and stood aside with it. "Not a thing. I was going to cover a story someone sent me about Evers Nealy opening a private prison off the south coast, but I couldn't find a second source to confirm it. I swear, that guy is slipperier than a Vaseline-soaked pollock."

"You're determined to take Nealy down one day, huh? You should get a job at *Panorama*."

He sipped his bitter brew and shook his head. "Higher you go, the blinder you get. You need to crawl in the mud to catch worms."

Craig stopped marching, checked his Fitbit with a raised eyebrow, and started pouring a coffee into a chipped and faded BEST DAD mug. "Yeah, well, I go wherever makes my mortgage payments easier."

"How is the family these days? Craig Junior doing okay?"

"My son's name is Taylor. You're going to remember that one of these days, I know it. He's fine anyway, thanks. Turns eight next week. I'm trying to get a week off work to go to Butlins."

Shane grimaced. "Lovely."

Craig blushed. "It has its charms. The entertainment's good – if you can find a seat – and the kids love it. Hey, while I have you, buddy, I was wondering if I could get your advice on something. I have an interview set up with that woman who claims to have two hearts, but she won't authorise her doctor to share her information with me."

"So you can't verify she's telling the truth?"

"No. Would you run with it anyway? I mean, it's just a fluff piece."

"You've been doing this long enough, Craig. What do you think you should do?"

"Probably can it, but it's a slow week."

Shane chewed the inside of his cheek for a moment, wondering how he could help. "I have a guy at the Office of National Statistics. I'll ask how many people in the UK are registered with the condition. If he tells me none, then you know she's lying. If he tells me one or more, then at least you know you're reporting on a legitimate phenomenon. Whether or not she's lying is then down to her. You can frame the piece around the condition and add her as an alleged sufferer."

"Yeah, you're right! That's what I'm going to do." He shook his head and chuckled. "How do you have so many contacts? I swear you have a guy everywhere."

"Blackmail, mostly."

Craig raised an eyebrow.

Shane chuckled. "I'm just straightforward with people. Tell them what you want and why you want it, and most people will be obliging, so long as they don't feel manipulated."

"Hmm, I don't think it's as easy as you make out. Last time I tried to purchase info from the police, I got arrested."

"I remember. It was my guy at the station who arranged for you to be let off with a caution."

"See what I mean? You're more connected than the Pope, yet you can't stand being around people most of the time."

"That's not true!" He actually felt a little unfairly judged by that. "I don't mind people, Craig. I just don't like to be bothered. Got my own shit going on, you know?"

Craig nodded thoughtfully. It looked like he was about to apologise for the unwarranted judgement, but Bernard's barking interrupted them. "Mogg, get in here," he yelled from his office.

Shane groaned. "Here we go. Good luck with your heart-lady."

"Thanks." Craig nodded towards Bernard's office. "Good luck to you too."

"If I'm not back in five minutes, delete my search history."

"Will do! Just as soon as I check it first."

Half a smile on his face, Shane headed for Bernard's office, slipping inside and sitting down without being asked. His boss was under a lot of pressure, but his problem had always been that he was too laid back. The man wanted an easy life, which Shane could respect, but it meant his underlings pretty much did whatever they liked. That had been even more of a problem back in the days when thirty-odd people had worked for the magazine, but it wasn't much better now with a skeleton crew of five. There weren't going to be any inspiring speeches or miraculous turnarounds, just an unstoppable slouch towards an ignominious ending. Shane felt sorry for the guy.

Bernard shook his head and grunted, but he was pale and sweaty rather than red with rage. "Can I rely on you, Shane?"

"As much as usual."

He leant forward and placed his elbows on his solid walnut desk – a gift from a celebrity footballer who'd been a fan of the magazine twelve years ago when fortunes had been different. It was the most expensive thing in the entire building and made Bernard look like an Iraqi dictator, especially with his long black beard and salt 'n' pepper sideburns. Admittedly, the spectacles and moth-eaten tie detracted from the look somewhat. "This is probably going to be our last few months working together," he said, "so I'd like us to give it our best. Let's go out with our heads held high, yes? We owe it to the magazine, and to each other."

Shane nodded. The thought of the mag shutting down saddened him more than he was willing to show, but he didn't see a reason to fall apart over it. You had to keep moving forward in life or the past would devour you. Maybe if he'd been with *Splatt!* since its formation twenty years ago like Bernard had, he would've felt different, but he'd seen *Splatt!*'s closure as inevitable for quite some time.

It won't kill me. Life goes on.

But Bernard was a sixty-year-old man who would likely never get an editor's job at another magazine. His experience was too niche and his methods too old-school. Hope existed that he might get in with a hobbyist publication or similar, but Shane could think of nothing worse than sourcing articles about model trains and tabletop gaming all day long. One of the greatest things about working at a bizarro magazine was that it was never dull. Headless zombie chickens one week, Walt Disney's cryogenically frozen head the next.

Shane placed his hands together in his lap and shifted in his seat. "I'm here as always, Bern. Not always on time, or in any fit shape to work, but I'm here. I care."

Bernard studied him through his specs, shook his head, then sighed. "Even on a bad day, you're a talented writer, Shane. Perhaps it's time for you to think about accomplishing what you're truly capable of. I can talk to head office about getting you moved to one of their other publications. Your past experience would go a long way. This was never where you belonged."

"Thanks."

"You know what I mean."

"You don't need to worry about me, boss. I'll be fine."

"I hope so, Shane, I really do. All I want is to leave this place knowing everyone is okay." He let his head drop, staring at his meaty hands out flat on the massive desk. "I've laid off so many people during the last few years it keeps me up at night."

"Nobody blames you for that." *Except for Brian. I've never seen anyone as angry as that guy was. He threw a pot plant out the window.*

"*I* blame me for that, Shane. Keeping this magazine afloat is my job, and I've all but failed."

"I'd say you've beaten the odds for twenty years. The magazine has just run its course. The world's changed, and people don't want to read about the 'Top Ten Tallest Human Beings' any more. They want to go online and have their existing viewpoints reinforced by a stream of mindless garbage. *Splatt!* is just another casualty of so-called progress. Progress that will see us all staring at screens twenty-four hours a day while eating processed bugs through bio-organic straws."

Bernard chuckled. "Makes me glad I'll be dead soon. Anyway, you got anything in the chamber? Who knows, maybe we can turn things around."

"Nothing yet, but I'll get on it. Haven't checked my emails over the weekend, so I'm sure there'll be something to work with."

Bernard slumped back in his seat, turned to his monitor, and started clicking his mouse. "Get to it then."

Shane gave a mock salute, got up, and left Bernard's office. He went straight into his own office and closed the door. As senior columnist, he had a decent space, with a window at the back and a small couch in the corner. His desk was positioned in the middle of the thin grey carpet, with ample room all around it as he didn't like to feel cornered. Instead of a computer, he had a laptop, although he rarely took it home. Once he left the office, work was done. In a world of 24/7 news, he was a 9-ish to 5 reporter.

When he slumped down onto his swivel chair, the uneven floor caused him to roll back several inches. He had to grab the edge of his desk and yank himself underneath. His laptop came to life as soon as he lifted the lid, still quick and responsive, mainly because he only used it for web surfing and office stuff.

As usual, he started his day by opening his emails. Among the usual junk and scams were a handful of unread emails from real-life humans. The first he opened was about an operational BT telephone box in the middle of a vast field. Why was it there? Who did the field belong to? The story had legs, and he could feature it as a side column, but as a main article...? No.

Then there was an email from a Devonshire fisherman who claimed to have caught a two-headed shark. Also not a big enough story for a main article. The third email, however, had a little more depth, and raised several questions.

FROM: Jesterness@everserve.com
  Subject: Kids are summoning th dead

. . .

Hello Mr Mogg

You have a magazine about stange things? You need to reporyt on this dangerous thing. Kids are summong the dead with that horrible app programme, Clip Switch. Have you seen it? It's gone trendy and Deaths are already ahappening. Look up dead girls in Nuneaton and then look up Nomon's Ritual. This is going to get worse.

Jester

Despite the typos, the email piqued Shane's interest enough to send a reply. It contained dead girls and rituals – a winning combination. "Okay," he said out loud. "I'll bite. Let's hop down this rabbit hole."

CHAPTER TWO

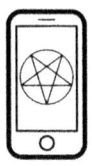

Shane typed "*Dead girls Nuneaton*" into the search bar and hit enter. Eversearch spat out the results immediately, starting with a ribbon of images that looked like screen caps taken from a mobile phone video. The first image featured two pouting young girls with shiny hair and pretty faces. The second showed those same girls standing further away from the camera, but one of them was doubled over in pain. The picture's tone was darker than the first, as if a shadow had crossed the lens.

Interesting. Need to track down the video these stills were taken fr—

Shane yelped as his office door sprang open and Craig appeared in the gap. His colleague looked at him expectantly. "Sorry, buddy. Did you call your guy at ONS?"

"What? Oh, not yet. I'll make the call now. Just give us five."

Craig thanked him and disappeared. Impatiently, Shane pulled out his mobile phone and called his contact, leaving a voicemail when the man failed to answer. He then sent Craig an email, letting him know he would get back to him about it once he got a reply. Finally, he replied to Rachel, who had messaged him complaining of a virus on her computer. He provided a link to some free online software that could help.

That girl is useless. How can a twenty-four-year-old not know how to deal with a computer virus?

Shane sat there for a moment, his hungover brain struggling to reconnect the synapses to remind him of what he'd been doing. "Right, two dead girls." He shook his head. "I really need to learn their names."

And so he did. Stefani Goodacre and Hannah Bridge. Both sixteen. Both dead after some kind of horrific incident two nights ago. No coroner's verdict had been rendered yet, but early reports suggested the girls had suffered a fatal reaction to taking illegal drugs.

Kids overdosing on pills was certainly worth reporting on, but it wasn't within Shane's purview. Regrettably, it didn't qualify as unusual or strange. In fact, it was depressingly normal.

But he wasn't done yet. Scanning further down the search results, he cast his eyes upon the various article headlines. The first few were stuffy and official, posted by the mainstream media, but halfway down was a report from an indie outlet called *Rhino News*. The headline read: *Girls perish after latest viral sensation turns deadly.*

"That's my McNugget." Shane clicked the link and opened the full article. It was a UK-based website, the article written last night by a reporter named Leighton Wong. It was highly speculative, but not without merit.

Wong alleged the girls had died after participating in a

new viral trend named "Nomon's Ritual". Said trend required a person to recite a brief passage of Latin text in front of a camera. The text was purportedly an ancient spell that would summon the dead. In the case of Hannah and Stefani, the spell had apparently worked.

Shane tutted to himself. "Bullshit."

He'd spent the last nine years chasing the oddities of life, but never had magic or ancient rituals been at the root of anything. Most stories were based around one of two things – unlikely probabilities or perversions of the norm. Guy wins the lottery three times in a row? Unlikely, but not witchcraft. Calf born with five legs? Perversion of a foetus in the womb. He reported on the improbable, not the impossible. The morbid, not the mystical.

And yet... he also had a duty to write about things that tickled people's fancies. It wasn't like he had anything else to write about.

"Okay. Let's keep this going. Where next?" He tapped his fingers on the desk, drumming out a rhythm while he thought things through. "Ah, of course."

He typed in the website address for Clip Switch, the scourge of today's youth. A billion users, all of them consuming footage of each other acting the fool. It seemed every other trend brought some new risk or outrageous behaviour. Kids swallowing hot chilli peppers and burning a hole in their stomachs? Check. People jumping out of moving vehicles to perform silly dances and breaking their ankles? Check. Idiots performing pranks and getting punched in the mouth for it? Check-check-check. Society was in free fall and Clip Switch was handing out faulty parachutes.

Shane searched up the dead girl's names and quickly found their channel: Stef&HanStuff. He clicked on their playlist and was perturbed to see two dozen thumbnails replaced with featureless grey stamps reading: <UNDER REVIEW>.

"Damn it. How do I get around this?" Clip Switch was one of the few places Shane didn't have "a guy".

He backed out and searched for the girl's names again. This time, he avoided clicking on their account and instead clicked on some of the related results. It took less than a minute to find what he needed. Nothing stayed hidden on the Internet.

"'Thank you, shameless re-posters."

Someone had saved and re-uploaded Stephanie and Hannah's controversial video to their own account. No doubt, Clip Switch would soon take it down, but for now it had avoided the site's censors. Shane double-clicked the video.

"Hey, my sexy friends, how ya doing? It's Stef here."

"And Han here."

"And we're about to... summon the dead."

Shane rolled his eyes. The one named Stef had her breasts unashamedly on display, and both girls were caked in makeup. They looked a lot older than sixteen, which he supposed was the point. He couldn't tell if they were having fun or if it was all just an act.

Grafting for those likes.

Stefani picked up a piece of old paper from a bed and read from it in an ominous voice. "*Con nomi segreti e porte nascoste, riporta i miei perduti e falli conoscere. Revia soul nocto. Revia soul nocto. Revia soul nocto. Amen.*"

Latin, for sure, but while Shane could recognise the dead language, he wasn't fluent in it. *Something about night? Souls?*

Spooky.

The other girl, Hannah, suddenly let out a bloodcurdling scream and clutched at her throat. It was unexpected enough that Shane jolted in his chair, but when he realised she was just pranking him, he grumbled irritably at his own gullibility.

Stefani grabbed Hannah by the arms and shouted in her face. "The power of Christ compels you. The power of Christ compels you!"

This is a trend? It's like a bad comedy skit. If I'd done anything so blasphemous as a kid, Mother would've locked me in my room for a year.

Hannah beamed at the camera while Stefani doubled over in hysterical laughter. "Don't forget to tag us in your own videos and share our channel. This is Han." She looked to her left. "This is Han!"

Stefani remained doubled over. She actually seemed to be in genuine distress, waving an arm in what looked like desperation.

Hannah's smile fell. "Stef, are you okay?"

Stefani fell to her knees, clawing at her throat. Her breasts almost spilled out of her top, but modesty seemed to be the farthest thing from her mind.

Shane wasn't sure if the two girls were acting.

But then something poured out of Stefani's mouth.

Beetles.

What the fudge?

Fat black bugs piled on the carpet, a writhing mass growing higher and higher.

The screen began to flicker and darken.

Shane leant forward, squinting to see better.

A lopsided face filled the screen, shrieking like a howling wind. The laptop's paltry speakers crackled under the abuse.

Shane threw himself backwards with a bellowed "fuck" and went rolling away from his desk in his chair.

Rachel burst into his office, scooping back her brown hair like she was ready for action. "Shane, what's wrong?"

He fumbled, unable to speak for a moment. "I, um, just lost a bet. It's fine."

"Jesus, you scared the life out of me. Are you sure you're okay?"

He looked at his laptop warily. "Yeah, I'm... I'm good."

She seemed to relax, her body loosening. "Can I get you a coffee?"

"Um, no." He nudged his mug on the desk. "I have one, but thanks."

"No problem. Give us a shout if you need anything." She flashed him a smile and left his office.

Shane sat, trembling for a moment, before gradually rolling himself back up to his desk. He was almost too afraid to touch his laptop again.

The video had ended on a black screen. A cleverly edited video?

Or something else?

Could a pair of sixteen-year-old girls have produced footage like that?

Those bugs pouring out of Stefani Goodacre's mouth looked pretty real.

And that shrieking face? What the hell was that?

Shane drilled down into the comments section to see what people were saying.

– Fake!

– This is so cool. How did they do it?

– A girl at my school did the ritual and now she's missing.

– This trend is so stupid.

– I would love to blow my load on them bazungas.

– Nice feet!

– Great content as always. I can't believe I actually made $1000 dollars today with crypto. And it was so easy! PM me and I'll show you how.

– Love you Stef and Han. More content please!!!

– I heard them is actually dead, yo. Look it up. For real!

– This is true, guys. They're really dead. You shouldn't mess with the dead.

– Shit... That was horrible. I just died!

Shane sat back in his seat, feeling a little spaced out from the unexpected fright. This story had legs, for sure, but he needed more than speculation and a video posted online. First, he needed to find out if the girls were skilled videographers. Could they have faked something like this? Also, how did they actually die? Was it a bad reaction to drugs, as early reports suggested, or was it something else?

Shane had several contacts on the police force. It was time to make use of them. He pulled out his mobile phone and made a call.

After making a few calls, Shane went and met Edwina at the McDonald's across the road. Ed was a freelance photojournalist at *Splatt!*, and probably the only person in Shane's life he almost considered a friend. She had been an employee at the magazine when Shane had first started working there, and had only gone freelance a couple of years ago when Bernard failed to meet her pay demands. No one begrudged her leaving. Her talent deserved more.

They shared a late breakfast while he briefed her on what he'd learned.

"So" – Ed propped her tattooed forearms on the tiny square table and raised her right eyebrow, the one with the stud piercing – "you think a ghost killed these girls?"

"No. I categorically do not believe that, Ed. I'm interested in the real reason two young girls dropped dead on the same night. My guy in the police said he has it on good authority that one girl had her neck snapped. Something happened in that bedroom, and I want to know what."

Ed wrinkled her nose. "It's a bit grim for *Splatt!*, don't you think? We usually do weird-shaped vegetables and celebrity lookalikes, not dead teenagers. Leave that to the true crime rags."

"Maybe you're right, but I've got nothing else in the chamber. Also, *Splatt!* is likely to go bust within months, so I need to go out on a high. If I cover this story, I can leverage it into something more mainstream when I inevitably have to look for a job. Can't let my last article be about a woman who's allergic to the colour yellow, can I?"

"No one will ever hire you, Shane. No one but Bernard can put up with you."

"We can't all be affirmative hires like you, Ed. What I would give to be a lesbian."

She plucked a piece of cheese from her meatless McMuffin and flicked it at him. "I'm sexually fluid, as you well know."

He grimaced and pulled the sticky yellow chunk out of his hair, plucking several long brown strands along with it. "Oh yeah, I forgot we slept together that one time. It was so forgettable."

"I would forget it if I could, but it was too traumatic. Eight years and it still feels so fresh, you know? My therapist says I might never heal from it."

Shane broke out in laughter. Few people could get a rise out of him like Ed. "So, you in or not? It's only an hour's drive away."

"Nuneaton? I'd say it's closer to two, but luckily for you, I'm free today. I just finished a project for *Country Home*. Christ. God, it was so boring. Curtain fabrics and wallpaper designs, bleurgh! Got to make rent somehow though, right? Can't go back to selling my body for spare change, can I? I promised my parents."

Shane examined the colourful anime tattoos on Ed's arms and neck, along with her short pink hair. "Curtains and wallpaper, huh? I would've thought that kind of thing was right up your alley."

"Yeah, you can shove it up my alley all right." She tossed down the remains of her McMuffin and wiped her mouth with the back of her hand. Then she let out a groan. "I can't tell you how much I miss sausage."

Shane offered her his sausage and bacon bap with ketchup. "So eat some. Why are you a vegetarian anyway?"

"I made the mistake of watching a documentary about cattle farming. Big mistake. Huge."

"Yeah, there's plenty to be said for non-enlightenment. You ready to go?"

"You have an address?"

Shane nodded. "My guy in the police."

"You and your contacts." She smirked. "I would love to know what you have on them."

"I write for a dying bizarro magazine that hasn't been popular since twenty ten. Most people don't see any risk in helping me. I'm not writing for *The Sun*."

Ed spat on the floor. "You named a tabloid. Pay up."

Rolling his eyes, Shane pulled some change out of his pocket and slid a pound across the table. "This is why I don't have friends."

"This is not why you don't have friends, Shane." She snatched up the pound and slotted it into the head of a plastic Labrador sitting behind her next to the doors. Then she turned back to face him. "It's because you have a deep-seated inability to trust other human beings."

"I trust *you*. Mostly. Sometimes."

She got up out of her seat, sipped the last of her water through a decaying paper straw, and smirked at him. "I'm honoured, but if I'm your only friend, you're in big trouble. Let people in, Shane. You'll find most of us aren't so bad."

He finished his Coke and stood up to leave with her. "If

life has taught me anything, it's that you're wrong. Do you want to drive or should I?"

"It's your gig. Put the miles on your car."

"Its value is already in the negative, so it'll be—" His phone rang in his pocket. He assumed it was his guy at the ONS getting back to him, but when he looked at the screen, he saw it was his sister. He muttered under his breath. "Not now, Sarah."

He went to cancel the call, but Ed grabbed his wrist. "Answer it. She's your sister!"

"Really? Okay, fine." With a harrumph, he answered the call and put the phone to his ear. "Go."

"I just got a call from the school," said Sarah, diving straight into a rant. "They said Evie was late last week too. If you can't be bothered to turn up on time, then—"

"She was a few minutes late, Sarah. So what? Teachers just like to complain. It's a power trip."

"Shane! It's the best school in the area and—"

"That *I* got Evie into."

She ignored that. "It's the best school in the area, and if Evie gets kicked out because of you, I swear to God you'll never see her again."

"Don't swear to God if you don't mean it, Sarah. What would Mother think?"

"Don't give me that. Just apologise."

"Apologise for what?" He glanced at Ed and saw her trying to listen in. She nodded at him, as if urging him to say sorry.

"Apologise for continually letting down your niece. You can screw up your own life, Shane, but not Evie's. She's had it hard enough without you teaching her bad habits."

"Sarah, I don't need this right now, okay?"

"Apologise."

"What?"

There was silence, followed by heavy breathing. "Apologise, Shane. I mean it."

"Don't threaten me."

"It's not a threat."

Sarah was his only family, but she was being unreasonable right now – and he wasn't about to put up with it. So he ended the call. "Bloody drama queen."

Ed gasped. "Did you just put the phone down on her?"

He put his phone back in his jeans pocket and shrugged. "So what?"

"You really want to die alone, don't you?"

"There are worse things." He yanked open one of the heavy glass doors and held it open. "Let's get to work. There are two dead girls calling our names."

"You're sick, do you know that?"

"I do know that, yes. You seem to like me anyway."

She barged past him, shaking her head and smirking. "I'm into a lot of things that are bad for me. But I gave up meat so I can give up you."

"Nah," he said, chuckling. "Some things are too hard to quit. I bet you'll be eating meat by the end of the day."

CHAPTER THREE

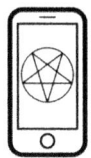

It turned out that neither of them had been right about the journey time. The trip from Redlake to Nuneaton, via Ed's portable satnav, took just over an hour and a half. They took Shane's Land Cruiser, which, despite its miles and three missing hubcaps, still ran well. The broken heaters were a pain, but eventually the engine heated the interior enough that they were at least no longer shivering. The rattling steering wheel was an altogether different concern, but as long as the car drove in a straight line, Shane saw no reason to make a fuss.

"There it is," said Ed, pointing ahead to a side road. She had a bottle of water in her hand and was screwing the cap back on. "Foxhole Avenue."

Shane pulled into a close of a dozen detached middle-class homes – not particularly large, but all with integrated garages and block-paved driveways. It was past noon on a Monday, so most of the driveways were empty.

The house they were searching for was easy to identify. Remnants of blue and white *POLICE* tape hung from its garage door and its front entrance, and a patch of lawn at the front had been trampled into mud. Number 6, Foxhole Avenue. Home of the Goodacre family.

It sent a shiver up Shane's spine to consider that two young girls had died here just two nights before.

"Looks like someone's home," said Ed, nodding out the window.

Shane nodded.

A blue Audi A4 sat in front of number six's garage, with a green wheelie bin perched behind its rear bumper, waiting to be returned to the house. Closed blinds covered the ground-floor windows, with no way to see inside.

Shane parked horizontally across the end of the driveway, blocking the blue Audi from reversing. He switched off the engine and sat there.

"You okay?" Ed asked.

"Just considering whether I really want to do this. Approach grieving parents about how their kid died."

"It's not very nice, but that's journalism. At least you care enough to be uncomfortable about it. Others don't."

He took a moment and decided that if Stefani's family asked him to leave, he would do so without argument. No badgering, no jamming his foot in the door. If they wanted him gone, he was gone.

"Okay, let's get this over with." He stepped out and waited on the driveway for Ed to join him. Once she did, the two of them walked up to the white PVC front door. It had a glazed panel at the top with a stained-glass rose. Shane raised his fist, hesitated, then knocked twice on the glass. When no one came to the door, he pressed a small button on the door frame. A jaunty bell sounded.

Still no one came.

"Okay, maybe they're out," said Ed, changing her initial assumption. "Probably gone to stay with friends or family. I wouldn't want to stay here either after—"

She shut up as a silhouette appeared behind the stained glass. Shane realised then that the door had a spy hole. He waved a hand and smiled. It felt inappropriate.

The rattling sound of a chain being released.

The door swung open a little.

A woman in her forties peered out at them through the gap with bleary, grey eyes. "Hello?"

Shane had to lick his lips to find his voice. "Um, hello there. Are you... Mrs Goodacre?"

"Miss Goodacre. I'm not married."

"Oh, okay, sorry about that. I was wondering if it would be okay to speak with you for a few minutes?"

"About Stefani?"

Shane swallowed a lump in his throat. Grief wafted from this woman like fumes. He shouldn't be there, on her doorstep, asking about things that were none of his business.

This was a bad idea.

Ed must have seen he was struggling because she took over. "We work for a magazine, Miss Goodacre. We're writing an article about the dangers of Internet trends and social media sites. I know it must be extremely painful, but we just wanted to ask if your daughter's death was in any way related to her online activity."

The woman let out a humourless chuckle. "Everything in Stef's life was related to her online activity. She posted everything on that stupid video site. I tried to keep her off it, but it was like an addiction. All she ever spoke about was numbers. Followers, views, likes, ad revenue." Fresh tears formed in her eyes. "At some point she stopped being my little girl, and I wasn't even paying attention. Her whole life was a performance for strangers on the Internet. A business. I don't even know who she really was."

Shane sighed. It was a story likely to be repeated by countless distraught parents. Social media had taken away their children, brainwashing them and turning them into performing monkeys. Engagement at all costs. Consume-consume-consume.

"That fucking sucks," said Shane before he could stop himself. "Sorry. I... I just think Internet giants like Clip Switch have a lot to answer for."

Miss Goodacre smiled, and it actually seemed genuine despite her obvious sadness. "No argument there, but it's me who's to blame. I should've been firmer with Stef, taught her better. Being a single parent's no picnic, but I could've done more. I could have."

Ed put a hand on the door, as if she wished to reach out and comfort the woman. "It's natural to blame yourself, Miss Goodacre. Do you... do you know what happened to your daughter? There's a report online about her performing some kind of ritual."

"An online trend," said Shane, nodding gently. "Do you know anything about it?"

Miss Goodacre opened the door an inch wider, signalling that her guard was lowering. To Shane's relief, she seemed willing to talk, apparently not upset by their questions at all. The glazed expression on her face, and the moistness of her eyes, suggested she was most likely still in shock from it all. Talking probably helped a little – gave her a moment's respite from her own mind.

"The police think I did it," she said, showing her teeth. "That I went berserk and killed them both. They won't believe the truth."

"So the police are still investigating?" asked Shane.

"They're here so often I should start charging 'em rent." She chuckled, but it was a miserable sound. "My Stef's bedroom is all locked up. I can't even go in there. My own daughter's room."

"That's terrible," said Shane. "What actually happened? You said the police won't believe the truth? What is the truth?"

She shook her head and stared off into space. "If I'd known Stef was getting involved in black magic, I would've stopped her. I didn't think she would be so stupid. That silly, silly girl."

"Are you talking about the ritual?" said Ed. "You know about it?"

"The police showed me the video. I had no idea."

Shane frowned. "Do you think the ritual contributed to what happened?"

"Of course it did!" Her bleary eyes went wide. "She summoned the dead. She brought back a monster who tore her apart from the inside out and snapped poor Hannah's neck like a twig."

Shane couldn't find his voice, too confused by what Miss Goodacre had just said. He took a moment to digest. Was she insane?

Ed removed her hand from the door and took a step back. "What are you telling us, Miss Goodacre?"

The grieving mother suddenly transformed. She turned feral. Angry. Unhinged. "That bastard took my daughter to pay me back for what I did."

"Who?"

"My brother!"

Ed folded her arms, tattoos blending together in a tapestry of faded reds and greens. "I don't understand. Y-your brother is responsible for what happened to your daughter?"

"He finally got his revenge." Miss Goodacre blinked slowly, and she seemed to look right through them. It was then that Shane smelled the booze. "I killed my younger brother twenty years ago," she muttered, "on his eighteenth birthday. We went to a club together to celebrate. I was supposed to stay sober and drive, but I gave in and had a few too many. Maybe if I hadn't been drunk I would've seen the fox sooner. Instead, I skidded right into a brick wall trying to avoid it. Anthony was in the passenger seat. His head was crushed like a lemon, but before he died, he looked at me for a second, and I swear all I saw was hatred. He blamed me for his death, so he came back to take my little girl away."

Shane finally found the ability to speak, although it took great effort. "W-what makes you think your brother came back from the dead to punish you?"

She huffed, as if it should've been obvious. "He told me! Right after killing my poor Stef, the bastard came to gloat. Now he won't leave me alone. He whispers in my ear when I try to sleep. He laughs when I cry. Eventually he'll kill me too." Her eyes sparkled with insanity. Her head tilted like her neck was broken. "Can you help? Is that why you're here?"

Shane grabbed Ed and stumbled backwards. The woman was mad with grief. It was understandable, even tragic, but the crazed look in her eyes chilled his blood. How had he missed it?

Miss Goodacre opened the door wide and revealed what she was wearing – a bloody night dress. She had clawed at her neck and chest, gouging bloody trails in her flesh. Her arms were purple with bruises and crescent-shaped bite marks. "He's getting his revenge," she yelled at them. "My daughter never should have said those words. She summoned the dead, and the dead are always angry. Do you hear me? They're always angry."

Shane kept on backing down the driveway with Ed beside him. "O-okay, Miss Goodacre. S-sorry for bothering you. We'll leave you in peace."

"We're so sorry for your loss," said Ed. "So sorry."

When they reached the end of the drive, Shane turned around and collided with the empty wheelie bin, almost knocking it – and himself – over. He let out a yelp and hurried to the driver's side door of his Land Cruiser, thanking God he hadn't locked it. He jumped inside, Ed only a second behind him.

"Fuck!" she said, stamping her Doc Martens in the passenger footwell. "What the fuck was that!"

Miss Goodacre stood in the doorway, yelling furiously at them. Nonsense. Madness. Grief. Terror.

Shane's hand trembled as he turned the key and started the engine. "We're getting the hell out of here." He was unsure why he was shouting, but he couldn't seem to lower his voice. "Then we're calling someone to come and help that woman."

"She's lost the plot," said Ed, her face turning pale.

"This was a bad idea."

"No shit! Come on, in case she comes after us."

Shane pulled the car away from the driveway and started to turn around in the street. As he did so, a teenage girl appeared in front of them. She was standing on the driveway of a house opposite. Clearly, she'd been watching them, but now that she'd been spotted, she turned and fled back inside the house.

"Who the hell is she?" asked Ed. "She was watching us."

Shane peered in his rear-view mirror to see if Miss Goodacre was chasing them. She wasn't. In fact, she'd gone back inside. It allowed him to take a pause and breathe. His heart was beating like a bongo, and he wanted to wail from the shock of it all, but slowly he calmed down. "I-I don't know who she is, but she might've known Stefani and Hannah. She looked about the same age, right?"

Ed's eyes bulged. "You want to carry this on?"

He let out a long sigh as his Land Cruiser idled in the middle of the road. "We're supposed to report on the strange and bizarre. I think this qualifies, don't you?"

Ed took a moment, but eventually she nodded with an exasperated sigh. "You're right. There're questions to be asked here, so I guess we should go ask them. Let's find out why that girl is so interested in us."

Shane was too shaken to keep talking, so he just looked Ed in the eye and nodded. Then he pulled up onto the driveway of the new house, which was number seven. He doubted it would be lucky.

Before he got out of the car, he called the local police station and asked them to perform a welfare check on Miss Goodacre.

That woman needs help!

Shane got out of the car and marched up to the front door, glancing back across the road at number six to reconfirm that Miss Goodacre was still indoors. The feral look in the woman's eyes would stay with him forever.

Does she really think she's being haunted by a ghost that killed her daughter?

A brother back for revenge?

Ed joined Shane at the front door. "Should I fetch my camera out of the boot?"

"Not yet." He pressed the doorbell.

A plain-looking girl opened the door. "Hey," she said, as if she'd known they were coming. "You're here about Stef and Han?"

Shane nodded. "We're journalists. Shane Mogg and Edwina Hobbs. Are you okay with answering some questions?"

The girl shrugged. She seemed a little out of it. "I guess."

"Can you start by telling us your name and age?"

"Millie LeRoux, sixteen. Am... am I going to die?"

"What are you talking about?" Ed stepped forward so that she was a half-step in front of Shane. "Why do you think you're going to die?"

"Because I did the ritual. The same one Stefani and

Hannah did. That's why they died, right?" She said it matter-of-factly, seemingly in a daze.

"No," said Ed, shaking her head vehemently. "We're trying to find out the reason they died, but it's certainly not because of a video they shared on Clip Switch."

Shane felt a shiver up his spine. He rubbed his hands together to comfort himself, a habit he'd kept from the days when he had regularly prayed. "Millie, did you know Stefani and Hannah very well?"

The girl leant against the door frame, hugging it. She wore baggy jeans and a scruffy orange jumper covered in places in what was most likely cat hair. "We all go to the same school. They..." She shrugged. "We've never really been friends."

"They were mean girls?" said Ed, offering a thin-lipped smile. "Pretty and popular? Yeah, I went to school with girls like that too."

Millie looked away, like she was ashamed to speak ill of the dead. "Sometimes they talked to me, but mostly they were just nasty. I didn't want them to die though."

"Of course not," said Ed. "We know that."

Ed had taken on the role of confidante, so Shane decided to concentrate on asking questions. "Do you have any idea what happened to Stefani and Hannah?"

The girl didn't hesitate. "I told you. It was the ritual. They summoned the dead."

"You really believe that?"

"Yes, I believe it! That's why I'm freaking out. I never should've done it. Now I'm gonna die."

Ed shook her head. "Why do you think you're going to die? Because you said some words on camera?"

"That's insane," said Shane. "You can't really bel—"

"My grandma came back."

Shane stopped speaking, his tongue a dead fish in his mouth. Ed stood silently beside him for a moment, but she was eventually able to give a reply. "D-did you just say your grandma came back? You mean, from the dead?"

Millie nodded. She didn't seem embarrassed or confused, only earnest and afraid. "It started last night. I woke up, and she was sitting on my bed, stroking my hair. She shushed me back to sleep, and then this morning I thought I'd been dreaming, but then I found her sitting inside my wardrobe."

Shane and Ed glanced at each other. They had worked on hundreds of stories together, but he doubted she would disagree that this was the strangest. First, Miss Goodacre, and now this young girl, both claiming ghosts were real. Was it some kind of group psychosis? Had a gas mains burst beneath the road and was now slowly intoxicating the residents of Foxhole Avenue?

"Could we meet your grandma?" asked Shane.

"She's gone," said Millie. "That's why I was out in the street. I was looking for her."

"Is your grandma not in your wardrobe any more, then?" asked Shane.

"No. She disappeared after breakfast this morning."

Ed folded her arms and let out a sigh. "Honey, do you think maybe you've just freaked yourself out because of what happened across the road? Two of the girls from your school dying so suddenly... It must be a lot to deal with."

Millie sneered, clearly offended. "You think I'm crazy? I'm not. Ghosts aren't supposed to be real, I get that. But they are! The ritual summons them – and I did the ritual. I said the words."

"Where did the ritual come from?" asked Shane. His hands were cold and trembling, so he shoved them in the pockets of his jeans. "Who started it?"

"I dunno. It just kind of appeared. Then everyone at school was doing it. Same as the Wednesday Addams dance."

Shane cleared his throat. "So you can't prove what you're telling us?"

"Do I need to?"

"Of course not." Ed offered a soft smile. "I have a question though. You think that you're going to die, right?"

Millie nodded, her bottom lip quivering.

"But you said it's your grandmother who came back. Why would she hurt you?"

"Grandma had a heart attack when I was ten, but I still remember her. She's not the same. Something's different. The way she looks at me... It's like when my cat spies a mouse in the grass. Her pupils get really big and they lock onto me. I think Grandma's hungry, but she won't eat when I offer her food."

"You think she's going to hurt you?" Ed chewed at her lip. This actually seemed to be getting to her. Was she buying into this?

It's insane. Ten years on this job and we've never found anything paranormal. Not even close.

Shane suddenly grew concerned about the girl's young age. "Millie, are you going to be okay? Should we speak with your parents? Your teachers? Clearly you're dealing with something right now."

She tutted and looked away. "You don't believe me."

"We're not saying that," Ed assured her. "We just want to be sure you're okay."

"My mum and dad are both at work. I told them I was too sick to go to school because I didn't get enough sleep. Tell you the truth, I wish I'd gone in. I don't want to be here alone."

Shane wasn't sure there was much to be gained from continuing this conversation – the girl wasn't in her right mind – yet he felt responsible now that they had her talking. "Millie? Do you need to get out of the house for an hour? We can go buy you lunch somewhere. Maybe try to make a little more sense of this."

Ed smiled and nodded. "Nothing official or anything like that. Just a chat."

"You'll pay?" asked Millie. "For food?"

"The magazine will pay," said Shane. "You ever heard of *Splatt!*?"

"Nope."

"Well, never mind. You want lunch or not?"

She nodded. "Okay, I know a place. You're not, like, going to abduct me or anything?"

Ed chuckled. "You're perfectly safe with us. Is the place far? We can walk if you'd like?"

"Yeah, we can walk. Just let me get my coat."

While they were waiting, Ed turned to Shane. "Should we be questioning a kid without her parents? I mean, I know she's sixteen, but still..."

"Eh, what's the worst that can happen? The magazine will be out of business before it ever gets in front of a judge."

"Good point. Still, you should probably try to be on your best behaviour."

He considered making a quip, but Ed's expression didn't seem like she was in the mood to joke. Come to think of it, neither was he.

CHAPTER FOUR

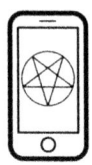

The place where Millie took them was a fish and chip shop about fifteen minutes away by foot. It had a lunchtime special – chip butties for three quid. Shane hadn't realised how hungry he was, but he wolfed down the buttery bread and chips so quick that it made his throat hurt. His McDonald's breakfast clearly hadn't touched the sides.

Millie ate more slowly, picking at her chips one by one and leaving the bread to the side of her plate. Ed ate a packet of prawn cocktail crisps, apparently watching her weight despite already being thin.

"So, Millie," said Shane, "when did you perform the ritual?"

"Saturday night. The same night Stef and Han died. Everyone was talking about it at school Friday, so I think a lot of us did it over the weekend."

"Has anybody else been hurt that you know of?"

She picked at another chip. "I don't really talk to many people, but I haven't heard anything."

"Stefani and Hannah apparently died right after filming their video. You're okay though. Why the difference?"

She shrugged. "Maybe the spirit they summoned was evil. My grandma was kind when she was alive, so she might be trying not to hurt me."

"Or maybe she doesn't intend to hurt you at all," said Ed, salty crumbs on her pierced bottom lip. "You said she was stroking your hair while you were sleeping, right? Sounds pretty loving to me."

Shane side-eyed Ed, wondering if she was humouring the girl, or if she actually believed her.

Millie popped a chip into her mouth and spoke around it. "Like I said, my grandma isn't right. It's like a part of her is missing or something. There's a hole in her."

Shane swallowed another mouthful of bread and chips before easing back his chair, scraping the legs against the tiles. "Your video on Clip Switch was normal, wasn't it? Nothing strange happened like it did with Stefani and Hannah?"

"You mean the bugs? No, nothing like that."

Ed propped an elbow on the table and ran a finger up and down her chin. "Can we watch your video, Millie?"

"Sure." Reaching into her pocket, Millie pulled out an android phone with an impressively big screen. Pokémon stickers adorned its rear case, but Shane could only name Pikachu. She woke the screen and loaded up the Clip Switch app, then selected a video clip from her library and played it.

The routine was identical to Stefani and Hannah's, except far less enthusiastic. Rather than read from a piece of paper, Millie was obviously looking at something off camera, perhaps a whiteboard or poster. She wore a fluffy purple onesie with a unicorn hood and was standing at the foot of a single bed. From the speed at which she recited the ritual, it was clear she was nervous in front of the camera. There was no pleasure or amusement in what she was doing. Only peer pressure.

In my day, peer pressure made you take up smoking or drinking. Now, it leads to public humiliation.

Unlike Stefani and Hannah's video, nothing bizarre happened in this one. Millie finished the ritual, stood there awkwardly, then rushed over to the camera to switch it off.

Shane looked up at the girl and saw her blushing. "This is what all the kids are doing?" he asked. "Why?"

"I dunno. To get views, I suppose. Trends get better numbers."

"And what do numbers get you? Fame? Money?"

"Stef and Han made money from their channel. They were always showing off their jewellery and clothes and stuff."

Ed tutted. "The Internet is the new casting couch. You still get fucked, but now it's less obvious."

Millie blushed even more, and Shane noticed she had very fine freckles over the bridge of her nose. She looked down at the table and shrugged. "Adults don't get it."

Shane agreed, but he saw no reason to embarrass the girl further. "Do you mind if I watch it one more time, Millie?"

She nudged the phone back across the table.

Shane watched the video again, this time paying more attention to the background details. The bedroom was cute, filled with stuffed toys and girly decorations. A small fish tank took up one corner, a nano cube with a bright LED light strip affixed to the top. "Nice fish," he commented. "I used to have an aquarium once."

"It's just a betta and a few neons. My mum got it to help with my anxiety. It calms me down."

"Yeah, fish have that effect."

"You suffer with anxiety a lot?" asked Ed.

She glanced down at her hands, twiddling her thumbs. "Sometimes. I worry."

"What about?"

"Everything."

Ed smiled. "Try yoga. It really helped me when I was dealing with some stuff at your age. Great for the waistline too."

"Okay."

Shane went back to watching the video. Other than the fish tank, the bed, and a side cabinet, there was very little else to see besides Millie. In fact, he was about to give up on the video when he noticed something towards the end. A sudden flicker. A sudden, minuscule change.

He dragged the clip back a few seconds and let it run again. He focused on the fish tank.

The light above the nano cube flickered, just for a second, and a strange reflection appeared on the glass. It was indistinct and with no obvious cause. Nothing else in the room had changed, but the atmosphere in the corner transformed ever so slightly. It corresponded with Millie saying the final few words of the ritual.

Is this it? The smoking gun? An artefact from the video editing software or some kind of filter?

"Huh, look at this." He showed Ed and Millie the disturbance. Ed frowned, unconvinced, but Millie scratched at the back of her head, tussling her mousy brown hair. She was the epitome of plain.

"Huh, I never noticed that," she said.

"Do you know how to edit videos, Millie? How about the kids at school? Vlogging is kind of a new religion, huh?"

She rolled her eyes at him. "I didn't edit the video. If you don't believe me, that's your problem."

"I'm not saying that. Just covering all the bases."

Ed nodded. "It's our job to ask questions, Millie. We don't mean any offence."

I do, thought Shane. *I want to get to the bottom of this.*

"Can you search up some more videos of people doing the ritual, please, Millie?" he asked. "Any random one will do."

Millie did a search and handed him back her phone. There were hundreds of results, each one a rectangular thumbnail with pouting teenagers either alone or in groups. He chose the third one, for no particular reason, and let it play. This video featured a topless young man dressed in white jogging bottoms. The focus was obviously supposed to be on his six-pack abs. Shane couldn't help but roll his eyes.

He skipped through the egotistical posturing and went right to the final few seconds of the boy performing the ritual.

Something happened.

The stainless steel light-rail on the ceiling flickered as the lad spoke the final few words of Latin. That was all. Barely noticeable.

Shane tried another video. This one was a trio of young girls, two thin and one dangerously obese. The larger girl was the ringleader, louder and more boisterous than her friends. When they finished the ritual, one of the slimmer girls suddenly had a gushing nosebleed.

He watched a third video, of a young man with apparent cerebral palsy reading the ritual from a notebook while leaning over a walking frame. He spoke the words in fits and starts, and the video ended with him falling to the floor face down while a shadow moved across the screen. Every video Shane watched featured either some subtle anomaly or something more overt like the boy falling or the girl with the nosebleed. The oddities always occurred in tandem with the final few words of the ritual being spoken.

"This is weird," said Shane. He shook his head and stared at the chips on his plate for a moment. Suddenly, his raging appetite had subsided. "Ed and I should really get going, but I want you to do something for me, please, Millie?"

Millie put a chip in her mouth and chewed. She tried to look him in the eye, but failed. "What is it?"

"If you see your grandma again, take some footage. Take a video of her and send it to me on my mobile. Do you have Wtrcooler?"

"The chat app? Yeah. I can send you a video on there. If my grandma comes back."

Or if she was ever there in the first place, he added internally.

Shane smiled. "And be safe. If you need anything at all, just give me a call."

"Thanks. To be honest, I feel better now that I've told someone. I tried to tell my parents, but they thought I was playing a prank on them. When Grandma next appears, I'm going to make them come take a look. See what they say then."

"Good plan," said Ed, beaming.

"Don't forget the video," said Shane. "I need proof. I need to figure out what the hell is going on."

Millie looked him in the eye. "You still don't believe me, do you?"

"That ghosts are real? No, I don't. Get me proof and maybe that will change."

She straightened up defiantly in her chair. "I will, and then you'll owe me an apology."

"Good luck," said Ed. "I've known this guy ten years, and he's never said the word sorry once."

"You'll get an apology," said Shane, ignoring Ed. "But first you need to get me proof." He stood up and wiped his hands on a paper napkin. If this was some kind of widespread prank, then he wanted to see what Millie would do next to reel him in.

Or she might provide him with proof, in which case the monopoly board of his mind would get flipped the fuck over and nothing would ever make sense again.

He prayed this was all just a prank.

Shane and Ed made it back to the Land Cruiser and were sitting inside. The analogue clock on the dashboard said half past two, and the weather was mild, so the car wasn't freezing any more, but Shane felt himself shivering all the same. For a few minutes, neither of them spoke, both digesting the information they had gathered.

It was pretty crazy.

Millie had gone somewhere else after leaving the chippie, and Shane couldn't help worrying about her. If he stuck to his assertion that what she was claiming couldn't possibly be true, then it meant she was mentally unwell or physically sick. Maybe she had swelling on the brain or a high-grade fever.

But she didn't look ill. She seemed completely sane, despite the madness of her claims.

Ed took out her phone and started scrolling Clip Switch. Again, they found more clips of kids performing the ritual. An endless source. They were like lemmings jumping off a cliff.

No, it's harmless, inane fun. Stefani and Hannah did nothing wrong, they were just kids. I need to find out what happened to them. Maybe it was Stefani's mum, like the police assume. It's usually a family member or a friend. I've watched enough Grim Tales *on YouTube to know that.*

"Some of these kids have millions of followers," said Ed, shaking her head in disbelief. "Fifteen-year-old girls flaunting themselves in front of God knows who. Look at this one."

Shane glanced over and saw a young girl, maybe only thirteen or fourteen, painting her toenails in front of the camera. The sight caused him to wince. "Gross. I hate feet."

"Yeah, me too, but obviously there's an audience out there that feels differently. It's prostitution."

"No, it's not." Shane cleared his throat, considering his

position. "It's crass, for sure, but if girls can make a living exploiting the weird fetishes of men, that's a win, isn't it?"

Ed blinked at him. "Wow, you're such a feminist. Young girls should aspire to more than this, Shane." She thrust her phone in front of his face.

He looked away. "Most *do* aspire to more. You just picked a bad video. These kids are just chasing popularity. It was no different in our day. The Internet has just turned a common character flaw into a billion-dollar industry. Narcissism is a career path now."

Ed nodded thoughtfully. "Not much different to journalism, I suppose. Always giving people your opinion, whether or not they asked for it, inserting yourself into their business."

"I was born to give people my unwanted opinion."

"Don't I know it!"

Shane smiled and let out a long, steadying breath. "Okay. Where do we go with this? We can probably proceed with what we have."

"You mean just write about the trend itself?"

He gripped the steering wheel, even though the car wasn't switched on. "I can add a healthy dose of speculation here, a few rumours there. It'll fly as an urban legend type piece."

"Will you mention Stefani and Hannah?"

"I suppose I should, but I don't want to be insensitive. Miss Goodacre didn't seem like she could take any more grief."

Ed fiddled with her eyebrow stud, something she often did when she was anxious or antsy. "I wonder if anyone went by to help her after we called."

"They said they would send someone as soon as they could, but who knows how long that means?" Shane stared out of the window at Miss Goodacre's house. It was dim inside. None of the lights were on. That wasn't concerning by itself, seeing as there was still daylight, but he had a horrible image of the woman lying in her bathtub dead, both wrists sliced open like blushed tomatoes. He shuddered again.

Then he saw her move past the window upstairs – a silhouette looking out at them before disappearing.

"She's inside," he said, relieved. "Probably best we leave her be. I'm sure there's family who will check in on her."

Like a long-dead brother.

Ed let out a long sigh. He asked her what she was thinking. "It just dredges up bad memories," she said. "I had a girlfriend who committed suicide in college. The week she died, she acted really strange. Calm, peaceful... Nothing like what you would think someone about to kill themselves would be."

"Shit, Ed. You never told me that."

She held up her left arm and showed a small tattoo on her wrist. It read: *Tabby*. "I don't like thinking about it. It's a cliche, but I've always blamed myself. She had a hard time accepting she was gay, but I pushed her into a relationship I don't think she was ready for. Then, when she was struggling, I never saw it in time to help her."

Shane looked her in the eye for a moment, but he couldn't maintain it. What was he supposed to say? "Ed, suicide is a collection of pain, and everybody only has so much shelf space for it. Whatever the reason your friend took her own life, I doubt it had as much to do with you as you think."

"I know. There's two parts to my mind. One part understands what you just said. The other will never be convinced. Guess that's part of being human."

Shane cleared his throat and sat up straight. "We're all at war with ourselves, I guess. Sometimes we lose."

Ed nodded thoughtfully and they both went back to sitting in silence inside the car. Ed went back to scrolling on her phone. She picked another video and watched it. A couple of minutes later, she gasped.

"What is it?" he asked, leaning over to see.

"Another weird one," she said. "Take a look."

She shared her screen and showed him a video of a boy and a girl, lovers by the way they touched each other and stood so close. The boy had short blond hair like vintage Eminem. The girl had an olive complexion and plump lips. They performed the ritual in tandem, their words forming a kind of harmony. Both had a professional manner, and their massive follower count suggested this wasn't their first donkey ride at the fair.

They were nearing the end of the ritual.

Shane tensed up.

And then he gasped, just like Ed had.

The two teenagers screamed as a dark figure leapt at them from off camera. The stranger wore dark blue, possibly overalls, and had inhumanly large hands. Before Shane could make out further detail, the screen went black. Ed played the clip back again and again. The stranger in overalls appeared every time, seeming to materialise off camera and take the teenagers completely by surprise.

"What the hell?" said Shane. "If this is a hoax, it's the world's most impressively organised hoax in history."

"Maybe kids are communicating through an app we don't know about, or some group on Reddit. Like that time everyone bought shares in GameStop to screw with Wall Street."

"Possibly. It's in bad taste though, don't you think? When people spontaneously unite on the Internet, it's usually for a good cause. This is sick though. Kids are dead."

"Oh no..." Ed's face wrinkled in horror. She was still staring at the screen and was now pointing to a comment underneath the video they'd just watched.

– Hey, I used to live down the street from these two. Jenna and Finn. They're a really nice couple and wouldn't fake something like this. Can someone check in on them and let us know they're okay, please? I'm worried. Their address is...

"Yikes," was all Shane could say.

Ed pulled a face. "This commenter just doxed those kids. Anyone might turn up at their house."

"What if *we* turn up?" suggested Shane.

"What do you mean?"

"I mean, so far we have Stefani and Hannah involved in some terrible tragedy after performing the ritual. If we go check on these new kids and something's happened to them..."

Ed nodded, pulling at her lip piercing with her teeth. "Then we have a second source to confirm."

"Or we find them alive and well, in which case we can call them out for their bullshit and put this thing to bed as a hoax."

"I don't like chasing down all these kids, Shane. It feels a bit icky."

"I agree, but sometimes this job involves getting icky. The address said Stroud, right? That's not a million miles away. We can probably be there in a couple hours, max. Besides, like you said, anyone could turn up. If there's trouble, we can help."

"Okay, fine, but this is the last swing at the piñata for me. It's too weird, and I've got enough on my plate already. I just want to go back to photographing curtains and bedspreads."

"I'll put a call in to *Good Housekeeping* personally for you. So, are we doing this?"

She breathed out through her nostrils, making them flare. "Shane, I really hope this is a hoax."

"Me too." He switched on the engine and pulled away from the kerb. Before he set off, he put his foot on the brake and looked at Ed. "What else do you have on your plate?"

"What?"

"You said you had enough on your plate. Like what?"

She looked away and sighed. "Nothing I want to bore you with. I just thought my life would be settled by forty. Instead, I'm single, living in a two-bedroom flat, and taking photographs of candelabras and table settings for a living. Not how I saw things going."

He nodded. "Life certainly has a way of kicking you in

the teeth, huh? At least it shouldn't be able to get any worse."

"Don't tempt fate," said Ed.

Shane gave her a smile and took his foot off the brake. "Me and fate are old enemies. Fate can go to hell."

He took off at speed.

CHAPTER FIVE

They made it to Stroud in just over an hour, speeding down the M42 followed by the M5. Late afternoons on a weekday were a good time to put another eighty miles on the clock. Traffic was quiet.

They followed the last directions on the satnav and ended up on a residential street much like any other. The houses were terraced, with a shared pavement area outside instead of driveways. A communal car park served the properties along with a row of ugly concrete garages with painted metal doors.

An ambulance sat on the pavement, blocking the path from one block of houses to the next. Its lights flashed silently while two female paramedics built like rugby players wheeled a blanket-covered body into the back.

"Shit," said Ed. "Do you think this is our young couple?"

Shane said nothing. The person on the trolley wasn't moving. It might even be a corpse. He'd once heard it on good authority that paramedics often avoided pronouncing people dead at a scene, preferring to bring flatlining patients into A&E to either give them one last slither of a chance, or to at least shift the burden of pronouncing death onto a doctor. It was also better than leaving a dead body in situ with a grieving family who might not be able to cope waiting for a coroner to arrive.

Shane pulled into the car park and switched off the engine. He and Ed got out and stood by the boot while she retrieved her camera. The way she held it in front of herself made it look like a shield, and perhaps she felt more comfortable being behind it.

Shane's legs felt hollow as they walked, and he had to put his hands out to steady himself.

They moved closer to the ambulance, slowly so that they could watch what was happening. Shane was sure the body on the trolley was dead. The blue blanket had been pulled up right beneath their chin. The only feature he could make out was a tangle of dark hair that looked wet.

Soaked in blood?

Ed kept her distance and snapped a few pics of the ambulance.

One of the paramedics glowered at Shane, probably assuming he was a gawper. "We're reporters," he assured her, but it didn't appear to improve her opinion of him. "Is this a young girl named Jenna? What happened?"

"I'm not talking to you," said the woman. "Please step back."

Shane nodded and did as she asked. Neither he nor Ed were in any mood to push things. If this casualty was indeed Jenna from the video, then the story had just become larger than they were equipped to handle. They weren't crime reporters. They were a pair of hacks coasting through life on an easy gig. He didn't want this. He'd given up serious journalism a long time ago.

And I never want to go back.

I just want to go home and get wasted. Then tomorrow I'll wake up with a hangover and pretend this day never happened.

Ed reached out and took his hand, spreading some of the warmth from her palm to his and letting her camera hang around her neck. "Hey, you okay? We're not doing anything wrong."

"Aren't we? It feels wrong."

"No, it just feels like something really bad is happening, and we don't know what to do about it."

He looked at her and nodded. "Should we leave?"

"I don't know. Maybe."

Shane was leaning heavily towards getting the hell out of there, but then he saw something that made him change his mind.

The boy. What's his name? Finn!

The boy from the video was alive. Not in good shape – sitting in a wheelchair with a blanket over his thighs – but not dead. An older woman pushed him along, her face awash with snot and tears. His mother perhaps?

Shane's legs moved of their own volition. A hot curiosity burned deep in his guts, and he knew he couldn't just go home and forget about this. Something was happening, and kids were getting hurt. He might be a hack at a failing bizarro magazine, but he was still a journalist. If he took what he did at all seriously, then he had to find answers for what was going on here.

Ed looked at Shane and gave a small nod, communicating that she was also past the point of no return. They were in this now. Together.

No longer willing to stand back, Shane stepped up onto the pavement and moved to meet the boy in the wheelchair. The woman pushing the boy looked at him through glazed eyes. "W-who are you?" she asked.

"My name's Shane Mogg. I'm a journalist looking into a spate of recent accidents involving teenagers on Clip Switch."

"Let us pass," she said, although her voice was weak and lacked conviction.

But the boy lifted his head, alert, almost panicked. There was blood on his temple, staining his short blond hair, but it was unclear where or what his injuries were. "It was the ritual!" he yelled. "It's real. We shouldn't have done it. Jenna. Jenna. God no, Jenna."

"What happened?" asked Ed. "What happened to Jenna?"

"He killed her!"

The woman behind the wheelchair tried to manoeuvre around Shane, but he stayed with her. He knew he only had a small window of opportunity to get answers from this shell-shocked boy. "Who killed her, Finn? Tell me so I can help."

"It was Eric Krendle. Fucking Creepy Krendle. He was in my room. He tore Jenna apart. We-we brought him back. It was my idea. I did this!"

"I told you to get back." Shane turned around and saw the paramedic marching towards him, a finger pointed at his face. "Do I need to call the police, sir?"

He shook his head and put his hands up in supplication. "No, I'm sorry. I'm just trying to find out what happened."

"Move!"

Ed took his arm. "Come on, Shane. We have what we need."

"Do we?"

"We have a name."

Shane back-pedalled, glancing at Finn and wondering if he should ask more questions. But the boy was already fading, slipping into shock; the trauma dragging him into an icy pit with its jagged fingernails. So he turned with Ed and headed back towards the ambulance and the car park. He was doing nothing illegal, but he didn't doubt the paramedic would call the police if he refused to leave.

As they hurried, Ed pulled on Shane's arm and altered their course. She took him right alongside the ambulance's rear bay. Close enough to peer inside.

Jesus Christ.

Shane's stomach turned. He didn't know if Jenna was alive or dead, but her face had been torn apart like wet tissue paper, exposing the skeletal protuberance of her left eye socket and the dull grey sheen of her cheekbone. She barely looked human. A paramedic sat beside her, back turned to the doors. They were doing nothing – which spoke volumes.

There's nothing they can *do.*

Shane felt himself wanting to puke, so he hurried away from the ambulance and bent over in the car park, taking deep breaths. Ed stroked his back until he trusted his diaphragm enough to let him stand.

"Come on," she said. "Let's go sit in the car."

He nodded, unable to speak. He wanted to collapse in a sobbing mess, affected by the horror on a primal level.

An innocent young girl mutilated.

Another one.

Sometimes, life was nothing but unfettered suffering, and all a person could do was look the other way and be glad it wasn't happening to them.

Ed took a few pictures, at a distance, of Finn being seen to, and then they both got back inside the car.

Haunted by the silence, Shane turned on the radio, pressing the number three button, which he'd tuned to an easy listening station. Ironically, the same Harry Styles song he'd listened to with Evie that morning was playing. The volume was low, but he chose not to increase it. A headache was fast approaching.

"We got a name to work with," said Ed, sitting in the passenger seat. "Shall I look it up?"

He frowned at her. "Huh?"

"Eric Krendle. That's what Finn said, right? He said Eric Krendle hurt Jenna."

"Did you see her face? It looked like a leopard attacked her."

"I saw it. It makes no sense, which is why we need to find answers." She pulled out her phone and unlocked the screen, speaking out loud as she tapped her finger. "Eric... Krendle... Here we go!"

He turned to her, a little lightheaded and still nauseous. "What have you got?"

"Well, not answers exactly. More like a bunch more questions. It says here that Eric Krendle was a school caretaker at a place near here. He abducted a twelve-year-old girl and held her at his home for five weeks." She pulled a face as she read on further, letting out a breath slowly. "Jeez, Shane. This guy was bad. He did awful things to this girl before strangling her to death. Police caught him when he tried to abduct a second girl and failed. They found the first girl rotting in his bed."

Shane put a hand to his stomach. "Jesus, I think I remember that all being in the newspapers all those years back. What kind of mental illness can make a man do something like that?"

"Hell if I know. Crossed wiring in the brain?"

"But this Eric Krendle is alive though, right? In prison?"

She looked at him and sighed, letting him know his statement was incorrect. "Shane, it says here he died eighteen months ago after serving two years of a life sentence, stabbed to death while on gardening duty by another prisoner, Errol Abiola."

Shane put a hand over his face and leant forward. "What is going on? That kid wasn't guessing or trying to be funny. He was certain that this Eric Krendle was the one who hurt his girlfriend. I saw it in his eyes, the certainty."

"Just like Miss Goodacre was certain it was her brother who killed her daughter. Two separate people with nothing to do with each other."

"But it's impossible, Ed. Ghosts aren't real. They don't pop up and murder people. Don't you think the world would know if that were a thing? Piers Morgan would be all over it."

She grunted. "Pay up."

He reached into his pocket with a groan and produced a fifty pence piece. "Here. Don't spend it all at once."

Ed took the money and started to flip the coin back and forth between her fingers while she appeared to think about something. "I've worked at *Splatt!* for almost fifteen years, and I've never seen a shred of credible proof for the supernatural. A few things I haven't been able to explain, sure, but never concrete evidence of there being anything other than what we see right in front of us. And yet... something or someone is attacking these kids, Shane. Maybe we need to look into this ritual. It could be..."

"Don't say it! It's ridiculous."

"Are you really so sure? Can we truly discount it completely?" She lifted her phone and showed it to him. On it was a photograph of what must have been Eric Krendle. The hulking man wore blue prison overalls, and he had on an oversized pair of gardening gloves – giant hands. It was the same person they'd seen jump Jenna and Finn in the video.

Shane sat there for a moment, upset, afraid, and utterly confused. His emotions were horses on a carousel, passing by one after another. It was time to push the emergency stop button and regain control of things. "Can you find the words for the ritual? Is it on Clip Switch anywhere?"

"Good idea. We should get them translated. Okay, let me search for the words. Yeah, here it is. Look."

She played a video that simply showed the words in white on a black screen, along with a haunting background of tinkling piano music. Shane took the phone from her and held it in his lap, staring down at the text. Then he said the words out loud.

Ed's eyes bulged. Her mouth fell open in a gasp. Despite that, she didn't interrupt him, and within thirty seconds he had recited the entire ritual, finishing with a shrug.

"Shane, what did you just do?"

He handed her back the phone. "Proved ghosts aren't real. If they are, then I just summoned one, right? Well, let it appear." He turned around and glanced at the back seats, out of the side windows, down in the footwells. The only thing he saw was the ambulance pulling out of the road and driving away with its lights flashing.

No ghosts. No monsters.

Not yet.

Maybe I'll wake up tonight with my grandma stroking my hair. Or, even worse, my mother.

"I don't think you should've done that," said Ed. Some of the colour had drained from her cheeks, making her hair seem even pinker by contrast. "It's tempting fate."

"Ed, we're the adults here. We need to find proper answers. Are you still with me?"

"Of course, but if a ghost appears and rips your head off, you're on your own."

"That's fair." He pulled on his seatbelt and turned the key to start the engine.

It wouldn't turn over, bleating like a dying sheep.

Ed let out a groan. "That isn't a good sign."

"It's an old car, that's all." He tried again, and when it still failed to start, he had to admit it felt like more than simple bad luck. "We'll just give it a minute," he muttered. "It'll be fine."

. . .

Shane finally got the old Land Cruiser purring after a few minutes of trying, and his anxiety gradually went away. It was just an old car. With over a hundred-K on the clock, it'd only been a matter of time until it became terminally ill. Other men might have bought something newer, but Shane didn't see the point of spending money unnecessarily. The Land Cruiser got him from A to B, which was all a car needed to do.

He and Ed were now sitting in a Burger King off of the A419. Ed had thrown her moral outrage to the wind and was tucking into a chicken sandwich. Shane had chosen nuggets, unable to contemplate eating beef after the sight of Jenna's bloody face. He and Ed had both been checking the news for updates on the girl's condition, but nothing had come up yet. They had found very little about Stefani and Hannah either. In fact, even the original article by Leighton Wong had been unpublished, and the *Rhino News* website was currently suffering a 404 error. It reeked of suppression.

Ed put down her chicken sandwich after eating half and picked up a French fry. Instead of eating it, she waggled it up and down like a finger. "Shane, what if the ritual is real? You could be in danger."

He snorted, surprised to see her so worried. They had got themselves worked up earlier, but it was time to come back down to reality. "Seriously, Ed, relax. Nothing's happened. I'm fine. I had to prove it wasn't real, and I've done that. No ghosts. No demons. We drove here without a single incident."

"I know, but—"

"We freaked out, understandably. I, for one, will never

be the same after today. The things we've seen… It's a fucked-up series of events, and I'm sorry for dragging you into it."

"How did *you* get dragged into it?" she asked, her eyes narrowing.

"An email. Came from someone called Joker or… no, it was Jester. They told me about the ritual and asked me to search for Stefani and Hannah."

"You should try to meet with them. Maybe they know more."

He popped a fry in his mouth, chewed, and then nodded. "I will. Whatever I do next, it's going to be from the comfort of my office. I'm not cut out for murder and carnage."

"Me neither. I used to think I was pretty hardcore, but Marilyn Manson never prepared me for this shit. We're heading back then?"

"I think so. I have enough to work with. Perhaps I'll try to source a few details on the ritual and its meaning, send a few emails to people in the know, but no more tracking down teens off the net. It hasn't turned out well."

"I barely took any pictures. It was pointless bringing me along." She lifted her camera from its bag on the floor and set it on the table.

"It's never pointless bringing you along, Ed." He shrugged. "Besides, anything you could've taken would have been too obscene. I'll grab some stock images, maybe a few screen caps from Clip Switch. It'll be fine."

"Good, because I'm still charging you for my time."

"I expect nothing less."

She switched on the camera and stared at its LCD. A frown quickly fell upon her face.

"What is it?" he asked.

"The pictures I took are all screwed up. Look!"

She handed over her camera and Shane was careful not to drop it. It was heavy, professional, and definitely worth more than his car. The LCD had a picture loaded on it, a still of the scene back at the ambulance. Finn was in the wheelchair, being pushed along by his mother. There was a strange blur behind them, like a burn mark on the lens. "What is that?"

"No idea. There's no reason for it to be there. It's on all the pictures."

Shane squinted and tried to study the vague distortion. It was kind of in the shape of a person, but there were no distinguishing features. It reminded him of Millie's video and the subtle change in lighting. He switched to the other photos and saw the blur again and again, always behind Finn, moving wherever he moved.

He handed back the camera with a shrug. "Weird. Must have been the flashing lights on the ambulance or something."

She put the camera back inside its bag. "Yeah... Maybe."

For a moment they both just sat there. Shane stared out of the window at the cars coming and going, travellers and commuters taking a break from the motorway to eat or take a shit.

Living their normal lives. Nothing has changed for them. If ghosts were real, there would be anarchy.

Ed ran her fingertips over her tattooed forearms as she

seemed to dwell on something. She'd received a voicemail during the drive and had appeared troubled ever since. He didn't ask her about it because it wasn't his business, and if she wanted his opinion she would ask for it. Still, when she looked up at him a few minutes later, she seemed tired and weary. "You really think *Splatt!*'s going to go under?"

"Uh-huh. If we'd jumped to the web sooner, maybe we could've kept going, but we won't be able to build up viewership fast enough to pay the bills now."

"What will you do? Seriously?"

He pulled at his fingers, cracking his knuckles, while staring out the window. "Honestly, I don't know. Writing's all I'm good at."

Ed raised an eyebrow.

"Eh," he admitted. "It's all I'm capable of. Anyway, it's Bernard I worry about. Twenty years of his life ending like this. He must be terrified."

"He deserved a happy retirement. Poor guy. I'm going to miss him. I'm going to miss everyone." She sniffed and looked away, possibly a little teary-eyed. "I still think of *Splatt!* as my family, even though I take jobs elsewhere."

"What would that make Craig?"

"The annoying cousin you avoid at weddings."

"Yep, that sounds about right." Shane stood up from the table and rubbed his hands together. "Right, I'm ready to get back on the road. D'you need a minute?"

She wiped her hands on a napkin and balled it up. "I just need to go to the toilet. Meet you back at the car?"

"You peed when we first got here. Do we need to get you a potty?"

"It's my nerves. I'm like a sprinkler when I'm anxious."

"Don't be anxious. I'll see you in a minute. Don't forget to wash your hands."

He exited the services building and immediately leapt to one side as a husky dog tied to a lamppost started barking at him. When he glared back at it, the animal grew even more agitated, fixing its glacial blue eyes and hopping back and forth.

"Nice to meet you too."

Rather than further aggravate the hound, Shane picked up his pace and headed for the car park. Evening was getting ready to arrive, the sky a joyless grey.

Shane's Land Cruiser looked a sorry state sitting next to a brand-new hybrid Range Rover in an adjacent bay. Even so, he couldn't fathom dropping eighty grand on a car, even if he had it. Sliding into the driver's seat of his Land Cruiser was like putting on old slippers. He knew the vehicle intimately and trusted it like an appendage, despite its earlier spluttering. He probably would have to crash it before he got rid of it.

I really wish the heaters worked though.

Shane let out a shiver and waited for Ed, wondering how much he would see her once he took another job. They knew each other well but had never met outside of work. He always drank alone, where he could get as fucked up as he pleased without being judged or without embarrassing himself.

A man should set an example, provide for his family.
Yeah, Mother, I hear you already.

He pulled out his phone and brought up the contacts. For a while, he considered calling his sister. Putting the phone down on her hadn't been cool, but he hated people being on his case. Anyway, why did Sarah always act as though she had the right to criticise him? He owed her nothing.

I don't owe anybody anything.

He decided not to call his sister, mainly because he didn't know what he wanted to say. Instead, he sent a text to Bernard saying he was on his way back to the office. Then he listened to a voice message from his guy at the ONS. No one in the UK had two hearts. In fact, the condition almost certainly didn't exist.

Well, there you go, Craig. Your contact is a big stinking liar. What a surprise.

Over the years, Shane had dealt with hundreds of bogus stories. People claiming to be Jesus or Elvis or an alien named Doosie. He'd once dismissed a lady who claimed to have had an immaculate birth, when really she'd just been unfaithful to her Royal Navy husband. There was the old man who claimed to have helped Hitler escape his bunker when the Axis replaced him with a lookalike. Oh, and never would he forget the fraud-slash-pervert who claimed he could predict a person's death date by swallowing a sample of their hair. Shane had spent almost a decade reporting on the bizarre, but people were the true oddities. Everyone was different, and yet depressingly the same in so many ways. Selfish, insecure, violent, manipulative, vain. Only occasionally did he see kindness, strength, and courage. Those were the stories he longed to write about, the McNuggets amongst a sea of soggy carrot sticks. It was one of the reasons he hadn't remained a mainstream journalist. It was too depressing and required too much of himself.

The Land Cruiser bounced on its springs, yanking Shane away from his thoughts. He turned to greet Ed but was surprised to find that she wasn't there. Had something put weight on his car from the outside? Glancing around, he saw nothing. The Range Rover had pulled away, leaving the adjacent space empty.

Huh. I swear I just felt someone get in.

His knee bobbed up and down in the footwell. "Come on, Ed. I want to get out of here."

Although hesitant to admit it, he was growing anxious sitting by himself. Goosebumps rose along his arms, and his knee continued hopping in the footwell. To distract himself, he pulled out his phone and checked the news. Still nothing about dead teenagers, which led him to wonder if the mainstream news was merely slow in catching up, or if there were some kind of mutual hesitation about what exactly to report. Even a half-serious mention of ghosts would lead to ridicule for papers like the *Guardian* or the *Independent*. Even the *Sun* and the *Mirror* would be reticent to suggest ghosts were killing kids.

His phone display flickered. It was a cheap Samsung model, not above glitching, but the screen hadn't ever had problems. All the same, it continued to flicker now, even as he tapped at the glass with his index finger. "Don't you die on me," he warned. He hated having to visit the phone shop. They always tried to get him to up his contract to some stupid new phone he didn't need.

This one has eighty megapixels and folds in half.
Does folding in half make it better?
Erm...
No thanks then.

Shane put his phone away and placed his skull back against the headrest. He took a deep breath.

Something brushed his ear.

The car rocked on its suspension again.

"What the fuck?"

He spun around in his seat and stared into the back.

But there was nothing there.

He batted at his ear, certain something had touched it.

"Must have been a bug," he muttered.

Turning back around, he felt his heart beating in his chest. He was on edge, clearly, so he urged himself to calm down. The hangover, tiredness, and general trauma of the day weren't helping, but there was another forty minutes of driving ahead, so he needed to get himself together. "I must look like hell."

He reached for the rear-view mirror and angled it towards himself to check out the state of his face.

Someone else stared back at him.

"Fuck!" In a full-blown panic, he grabbed the door handle and tried to get out of the car. But the door was stuck. The Land Cruiser bounced on its springs like a fairground ride, but Shane didn't know if it was from his own flailing or something else. All he knew was that he wanted out of there.

He reached across the passenger seat and grabbed the other handle.

The door opened.

Shane yelped.

Ed looked in at him, confused. "Um, everything okay?"

"What? Did you...?" He straightened up and looked in the rear-view mirror again. This time, he saw only his own ashen skin and bleary eyes. Nothing was inside the car except for him. "It's nothing," he said. "I'm just freaking myself out. Too little sleep and too much excitement."

She slid onto the passenger seat but kept her eyes on him. Her concern was obvious, but she said nothing. What could she say?

He wasn't about to say anything either. It would only make him sound insane. "Y-you all empty?"

"Yeah. The toilets were gross."

"Well, women are disgusting."

Ed chuckled. "We actually are. Some of us treat public toilets like a poop party. God knows how people make such a mess."

"Best not to think about it. You ready?"

"Uh-huh." She frowned at him. "You sure you're all right, Shane? You look like you've seen a..." She stopped and cleared her throat. "Anything I can do?"

He shook his head at her. Bad choice of words.

"I'm fine." He started the engine. "Tickety-boo."

He tore out of the car park so fast that half a dozen drivers had to slam on their brakes and beep their horns. When he looked into the rear-view mirror, he asked himself if he had really seen who he thought he had.

No way. It's impossible.

CHAPTER SIX

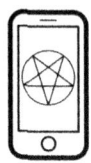

It felt good to get back to the office. Ed had gone home to shower and wash the day off, but Shane wanted to see people before retiring to the bottle, which was very out of character for him. It was a few minutes after five, but the office didn't empty until six-ish usually. The first person to greet him was Rachel.

She gave him a massive smile. "Oh hey, Shane. It's been quiet without you today. Did you get any good stories?"

"Just one, and I wouldn't call it good."

She smiled at him again, probably confused by his words or disturbed by the state of him. "Can I get you a coffee?"

"God yes. You're a star."

"Coming right up." She hurried off to the machine to go make him one, enthusiastic even at the end of her shift.

Oh, to be young again.

Shane crossed the floor to his office, but Craig cut him off.

"My guy got back to me," said Shane, putting a hand up

before his colleague could badger him. "Your lady's full of it."

His face fell. "Seriously? That's a downer. She really had me convinced."

"I don't know what to tell you, mate. No one in the UK has two hearts. Either she provides you with medical evidence or you cut her loose."

"Damn. Now I'll have to run with something else. You got anything spare?"

"Wish I did. Can't help you."

He let out a long, dramatic sigh. "Thanks anyway, Shane. I owe you one."

"I've lost count of how many you owe me. What's one more?"

Craig stormed off, muttering to himself. Even after years on the job, he still took it personally when people lied to him. Naivety was a bad thing for a journalist to have.

Shane entered his office and turned to close the door, but paused, reconsidered, and decided to leave it open. Before sitting down, he went over to the window and peered outside. His Land Cruiser was again parked next to Bernard's Alfa Romeo. Somehow, his car no longer felt like a cosy extension of himself. The experience back at the motorway services had left him wary of being inside it – especially alone.

Oh, come on, man. My car isn't haunted.

He slumped down in his chair, rolling away from his desk and having to yank himself forward. Huffing, he lifted the lid on his laptop, but the screen remained blank. The fan whirred to life, and it did the usual beepity-boop, but it took several seconds for the screen to wake up. Loading Windows took two whole minutes.

"Not you too. Why is all my technology playing up on me today?"

Because I buy cheap shit and use it until it falls apart.

Thriftiness is a virtue, child. Give not oneself to gluttony and want.

Shane chewed at his bottom lip and seethed for a few moments, feeling frustrated. His body cried out for a beer, his mind even more so, desperate to send this day spiralling into a fuzzy oblivion where nothing was as bad as it seemed.

Once his laptop finally woke up, Shane did what he always did first. He checked his emails.

A Nigerian charity worker was looking to move a large amount of money out of the country and needed his help.

A poorly formatted newsletter updated him about the gym he had quit three years ago.

An email from someone who wanted *Splatt!* to feature advertising for their new energy drink.

And a new email from Jester. Shane opened it immediately.

FROM: *Jesterness@everserve.com*
Subject: It's happening all over!

The email began not with a greeting, but with six hyperlinks. Each led to a Clip Switch video featuring young people performing the ritual. All ended badly, with the startled youths either being attacked by someone – or something – off camera, or suddenly falling ill with nosebleeds, choking fits, or even apparent heart attacks. In the last video, a lone girl opened her jaws so wide that they dislocated, and a gore-covered snake forced its way out of her bulging throat. It could all have been faked, but he didn't see how. Or why.

Perhaps Jester was the one behind the whole thing.

This is an attack on our youth. Someone has done tihs one purpose. Find the original video. Find out who is behind this terrorrism before it gets worse. I've tried to get help, but no one is listening. I hope you are.

Jester

Shane read the email twice more before sending off a reply asking to meet.

Until he got a response, he couldn't ignore Jester's suggestion of digging deeper. There was a dangling thread in front of his face begging to be pulled.

Who posted the original video?

Reluctantly, Shane loaded up Clip Switch, a website and app he'd come to loathe. Perhaps irrationally, he blamed it for the deaths of Stefani, Hannah, Jenna, and however many more. Freedom of the Internet had once seemed like an unimpeachable right. Now he wondered if too much freedom could be a bad thing.

He brought up the discovery bar and searched for *'Nomon's ritual original'*.

Dishearteningly, hundreds of videos came up in the results, mostly more youths performing the trend. He opened a few but clicked away early, not wanting to view their possibly grisly endings. Instead, he checked the comments, searching for information or reoccurring themes. Eventually, he found one. Several commenters mentioned the name Vita.

Shane performed another search: *Nomon's ritual Vita*.

This time, a mere dozen videos came up in the search results. One immediately caught his eye – an account with only a single video. The uploader's name was Vita. Not Vita23 or Vita_real. Just Vita.

Shane clicked on the video.

A figure dressed in a red satin robe with a cowl stepped in front of a grainy camera. It appeared to be inside a church, Shane based his assumption on the stone floors and walls, but it could also have been a castle or a ruin or maybe even a root cellar.

The man recited the ritual in fluent Latin, not reading the words but speaking them from memory. Words that were familiar and understood.

A scholar maybe? University lecturer? One who speaks Latin?

A monk?

The ritual was nearing its end. In the stranger's hands was a candle, and he peered down at the flame. The cowl cast his face in shadow, but the flickering light revealed age-sagged jowls and crow's feet. Probably a man, but he couldn't be certain.

Who are you? Why would you do this?

Do what? Am I saying I believe the ritual is real? No proof of that. None at all.

Have faith, child. Believe or be damned.

"Shut up, Mother," he said out loud, closing his eyes tightly and forcing the echoes of her away.

The stranger paused for a moment and seemed to mutter, speaking too quietly for Shane to make out his words. He then lifted his head high and recited the last part of the ritual.

Shane's eyes flickered as he anticipated something happening, but nothing did. The stranger simply turned and walked off-screen with their candle, leaving behind an empty stone chamber. There was a low noise or static, keeping the scene from silence.

Shane shook his head, wishing the video had given him more to work with. There was nothing to focus on, and no obvious way of identifying the stranger in the robe. Even if he could work out who they were, they hadn't exactly committed a crime.

He played the video again, waiting for the moment where the stranger muttered to himself, turning up the laptop's volume and listening carefully. The muttered words seemed to be more Latin, but spoken very, very softly. It wasn't a part of the ritual kids were reciting online – it was an extra line. Shane couldn't make it out, no matter how hard he tried. Even with the volume all the way up, the words were too quiet.

He slumped back in his chair. "Damn it."

The stranger walked off camera again, leaving behind the stone chamber. The static noise resumed.

No. That's not static. Is that...?

Cheering?

Shane rewound the clip and played the ending again. With the volume increased, the background noise was easier to recognise.

Definitely cheering.

In fact, it sounded like a large crowd.

Who is that, and why are they cheering?

More importantly: where *are they?*

Shane's hands trembled. He was gasping for a beer, but he wasn't so far gone as an alcoholic that he got the shakes. No, his hands were shaking because he was completely frazzled. He felt like a sighted person in a crowd full of the blind while an alligator stalked the room, snapping up bodies one by one. Why wasn't anybody else freaking out over what was happening? How did this all fall on him? Why could only he see?

Can I just walk away from this? Is it ethical?

Screw ethics, can I live with it? Can I walk away and just forget this?

His phone buzzed. A message from Evie.

Got in trouble with mum. Skipped out of school at lunchtime and she found out. She's driving me mental.

Shane closed his eyes and tipped his head back. He needed a moment of quiet, a few seconds of solitude to concentrate on his breathing.

Then he called Evie's phone.

She picked up immediately. "Uncle Shane? Will you

talk to her? I'm locked in my bedroom and she won't let me out. The mad bitch. She's totally overreacting. I... I can't be here all by myself. Will you talk to her?"

Shane couldn't help but smile at the sound of his rebellious niece, but he knew he had a duty to be an adult here. "She's just being a parent, Evie. It's her job to get on your back about these things. Education's important."

"Didn't you tell me the modern education system is designed to churn out mindless workers for the elite? Even if it wasn't, I'm not smart enough to do anything anyway, so what's the point?"

"I've met some pretty stupid doctors and teachers in my time, Evie, and you aren't stupid. Whatever you want to do in life, you can make it happen. But you have to put the work in and go to school."

"You sound like mum. You're supposed to be on my side, Uncle Shane."

"I am on your side – always. Look, I know your mum can be a pain, but she only wants what's best for you."

"How is turning off the Wi-Fi best for me? I can't do my homework without the Internet, can I?"

Shane chuckled. "I don't think that's really what you're concerned about, is it?"

She let out a sigh. "Hey, can I ask you something?"

"Shoot."

"You report on weird things, right? Do you ever find stuff that's, like, really... um..." She let out another sigh, sounding troubled. "Actually, forget it. It's stupid."

"You can tell me. What is it?"

"Nothing. Honestly. Just stupid school stuff."

Shane had a feeling this was another moment where he

should push further, but again he didn't know what to say. His gut told him something was wrong, but he didn't know if it was coming from Evie or from within himself. "Hey, Evie, do you know about this ritual kids are doing online?"

She paused a moment. "Ritual?"

"Yeah. Like a summoning the dead spell. Have you seen it?"

Another pause. "No."

"Evie, tell me the truth."

"I am."

He didn't know whether she was bullshitting him, but she had promised to always tell him the truth, so he needed to assume she was doing that now. "Okay. Look, if someone shares a video of a Latin ritual, promise you'll just delete it. And whatever you do, don't copy it yourself."

"Uncle Shane, I have to go."

"Why? What is it?"

"My mum. She's coming up the stairs. I'm not supposed to be on my phone. Speak soon."

"Evie? Evie, you there?"

The line went dead.

"Goddamn it."

Shane tossed his phone down on the desk and muttered to himself. He didn't believe the ritual was real, so why had he felt the need to warn his niece? All day long he'd done nothing but witness the aftermath of other people's misfortune. Perhaps it was better to be safe than sorry.

Craig popped his head into Shane's office. "It's six o'clock. I'm off."

Shane looked up, then waved a hand absent-mindedly. "Oh yeah, have a good night, mate."

Craig stayed where he was, a frown upon his face. "Are you staying? You're usually first out the door."

"Just finishing up. Been a long day, so what's another twenty minutes?"

"Was that your niece on the phone? I heard you say Evie. That's your sister's kid, right?"

Shane scowled. "You were listening in?"

"Your door was open and I came to say goodnight. I only heard you sounding concerned. Can I help?"

"I doubt it."

"Try me."

Shane gritted his teeth. The last thing he wanted was to share his personal life with Craig. *And yet...*

Maybe Ed's right, and I should give people a chance. Craig's not so bad.

"Evie's just going through a rebellious phase," he admitted. "The worst part is, I think she sees me as some kind of role model."

Craig nodded, his face serious. "I can see that. Makes sense."

"Why would anyone see me as a role model?"

"Most people go through life following the rules, even when it hurts them, but you don't give a shit – and I mean that in a good way. I see why a teenager might idolise you. Rebels are cool when you're young."

"I'm not a rebel."

Craig smirked, his eyes wrinkling at the corners, showing the first signs of ageing. "Most men your age are married, drowning in debt, with a bunch of kids hanging off them. Every rule society expected you to follow, you've sidestepped. You don't buy into any of it, do you?"

I used to. I once bought into it all.
And look where it got me.

"What's to buy into, Craig? I mean, people work till they drop, pay bills, pay taxes, obey a thousand different laws, but who the hell ever decided they have to do all that? Not me. Not anyone I know. We've put ourselves in cages, but all people need to do is say no and the system will change. No, I will not slave away so my boss can buy a bigger boat. No, I won't pay tax to a government that squanders it on wars and corporate subsidies. No, I won't pay a fine for public indecency after drinking an intoxicating substance that you freely sold to me for profit, knowing full well the damage it causes."

Craig frowned. "Hmm, that last one was pretty specific."

"It still stands. Who decided we have to live our lives a certain way? Nine out of ten people hate their jobs, yet they spend forty hours a week doing it. Why would we do that to ourselves as a species?" He stopped, inhaled deeply, and then let it out in a grunt. "See? This is why I don't open up. My innate cynicism takes ahold of the wheel."

"I agree, society isn't in great shape right now. But I don't have a clue how to change it, or what would be better. Most people just make do with what they have."

"And therein lies the problem." He cleared his throat and stretched out his arms in defeat. "Anyway, that doesn't help me with my problem. My niece wants to be a rebel, but I don't want her to hurt herself or hold herself back, even though I know the whole system is built on quicksand. Sometimes I worry my sister can't cope being a parent on her own."

"She's a single mum? Where's Dad?"

"God knows. I don't even think Sarah's sure who the donor was. She was a little... wild before Evie came along. I don't blame her. Our mother was hard to please. Religious, you know? Once Sarah left school, I think she just wanted to be free, so she broke every rule she could. Evie was just the last of her many mistakes. Now she turns her nose up at me and acts like I'm the one who should be ashamed. Hypocrite."

Craig smirked. "Sounds like your mum raised two rebels. At least your sister settled down once she had a kid. If she's struggling, you should help her."

"I do help her!"

Craig frowned, a questioning look on his puggish face.

Shane sighed. "Or maybe I don't. Fuck, I dunno. You think I need to get my act together?"

"I don't think you need to get your act together, but you don't have to be angry at your sister because she got hers together. Sounds like she didn't have much of a choice."

"You're probably right."

"You're a good bloke, Shane. If this place goes under, it's been a pleasure working with you."

"Really?"

"Eh, it's been tolerable."

"Thanks, Craig. We've never been for a drink, have we?"

"No, we haven't." He turned and left, whistling a tune to himself as he walked away.

Shane drummed his fingers on the desk and thought about calling his sister. But he didn't know what to say. So he just sat there, thinking.

He checked the news again and still found nothing. *Rhino News* was still failing to load. It led him to consider something. How had Leighton Wong found out about the ritual so quickly? And why had he taken down his article.

There was only one way to find out.

Shane checked out LinkedIn and found the journalist's contact details easily enough using *Splatt!*'s account and credentials. He picked up his phone and gave the guy a ring.

"Hello?"

Shane sat forward and propped his elbows on the desk. "Leighton Wong?"

"Yes. Who's this?"

"My name is Shane Mogg. I work at *Splatt!* Magazine."

"I've heard of it."

"Oh... well, that's refreshing."

"What do you want?"

Shane decided to waste no time. "Why did you take down your article about Stefani Goodacre and Hannah Bridge?"

"The website is down. Technical issues."

"Yeah, I noticed. Come on though, journo to journo, who made you pull it?"

"No one. It was a bad article. I never substantiated any of the details and it was poorly written. Click bait, you know? Why are you even calling me about it?"

Shane sighed. The guy didn't want to play ball, and Shane had zero leverage over him. Besides maybe appealing to the guy's conscience. "More kids have been hurt, Mr Wong. I've been following the story all day. Something's going on, and Nomon's Ritual seems to be connected. Of course, I'm not saying that it's gho—"

"It's real," said Leighton Wong. "The words are real. If I were you, I would drop the story and avoid getting caught in the fallout. We pulled the article because it was getting too many hits. Kids were reading about it on our website and then going off to do the ritual themselves. They're going to get hurt because of me."

Shane realised the man was drunk. He had a vaguely cockney accent, so he was probably writing out of London. While *Rhino News* was independent, it would still have its paymasters. "You're worried about getting sued."

"Not me. I don't give a shit. I just don't want kids finding out about the ritual because of my article. The magazine's owners ordered me to pull it, but I would have done it anyway."

"You really believe the ritual is real? How did you find out about it?"

He huffed down the phone. "Did you do any research on me? I'm literally a social media reporter. I write fluff pieces and click bait about the latest trends and memes. I haven't written a serious piece of journalism my entire life – until last night. It was only supposed to be a spooky story to get some clicks, but then I started seeing all the videos being posted on Clip Switch. Mr Mogg, no one is reporting on it, but kids are dying. It's happening right now."

"Look," Shane said, sighing, again feeling like the only sane person in the room. "Can we meet? I want to get to the bottom of this, but things keep getting out of hand. Ghosts aren't real. I know that because I performed the ritual myself and everything is fine. Nothing's happened."

"You performed the ritual?"

"Yes, this afternoon. I'm okay."

"No, you're not okay, Mr Mogg. Someone or something will be coming for you. I'm sorry, but don't contact me again. I want nothing to do with this."

The line went dead.

So did a part of Shane. When you were the only sane person in the room, how long until the crazy people started making sense? How long before the sane person became the one who was crazy?

Just relax. Everything's fine. The world is the same today as it was yesterday.

Don't lose a grip on what's real.

He leant on his desk and put his head in hands, taking deep breaths and trying to clear his mind. His head was full of static, just like the ending of Vita's video.

I need to call Ed. Tell her what I found.

By six fifteen, the office was empty of everyone except for Shane. The thought of going home unsettled him, but he had no place else to go. He didn't want to be alone, but drinking at a pub would be unbearable. Spending time with drunk people was the worst. They always over-shared.

Maybe I should've chased Craig and asked him for a drink.

He didn't seem keen. Am I an arsehole?

Yep, pretty much.

With no choice left but to leave, Shane switched off the lights and set the security alarm. He used his keys to lock up and then headed out to his car. The final, dying remnants of daylight cast everything in a grey gloom, and the thought of encroaching darkness caused him to shudder.

Someone or something will be coming for you.

You're not okay, Mr Mogg.

Someone stepped out from behind his Land Cruiser.

Shane leapt in the air and squealed. "Shit! Wh-who the hell are you?"

"Are you Mr Mogg?" asked the stranger, a tiny old lady with a short, auburn perm and an olive complexion. The canvass tote on her shoulder was half as big as she was, and the glittery crucifix over the breast of her green cardigan could have belonged to Jay-Z.

"Yes, that's me. You scared the hell out of me, lady."

"I'm sorry. My name's Gina D'Amata."

He drew a blank. "I'm sorry, who?"

"You know me as Jester. You wanted to meet. Well, here I am."

Shane stumbled back a step, lost for words. His day wasn't over yet.

CHAPTER SEVEN

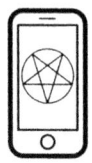

The first thing Shane did was call Ed. She didn't answer his call, but returned it two minutes later, having just got out of the shower. She wasn't eager to get dressed and go out, but he talked her into it. Understanding the ritual was important for their peace of mind.

Now he and Ed were both sitting inside *Splatt!*'s conference room with an old lady who claimed to be Jester.

Gina, it turned out, was an Italian national who had emigrated from Sicily to the United Kingdom thirty years ago with her Welsh opera singer husband who had sadly passed away in two-thousand-five from the ravages of stomach cancer. She'd been living alone ever since, surviving off a generous life insurance policy.

Shane fetched her a cup of tea and a plate of biscuits before offering her a seat around the conference room's large pine table. He declined to sit, too amped up and his head swimming with questions he wanted to ask. Ed seemed tired, and she was currently sitting at the side of the room, rubbing at her eyes with the heels of her palms.

"Why did you come here?" Shane asked Gina, to start things off.

"Because you asked me, dear," she replied with the faded remnants of an accent.

"Yes, but why did you agree? Do you have something you can offer me?"

She frowned. "Offer you? Like what?"

"I don't know. Some sanity, perhaps? This has been one hell of a crazy day, lady, and it all started with your email."

The woman did the sign of the cross, possibly as an overreaction to him mentioning hell. "I emailed dozens of people," she said. "We need to put a stop to this blasphemy before more innocent young people die. If I knew my way around a computer, I would try to do something about it myself."

"Such as?"

"I don't know. Hack that Clip Switch website, for one. Take it down."

Shane smirked. "I don't think it's that easy."

"Well, it should be. Is there no one in control of the Internet? Kids are dying, and nothing is being done."

Ed crossed her ankles and sat up straight, as if she were trying to keep herself awake. "We've been trying to do something about it all day, Gina, but we kept arriving too late. There's no way for us to know who's going to be in danger next. You can't stop a trend."

Shane nodded. "You just have to wait for it to die out."

Gina grimaced. "Poor choice of words, Mr Mogg. So how many have to die for people to take notice? What are parents doing, letting their kids cavort on the Internet without supervision?"

"It's not the nineteen fifties," said Shane. "Times have changed."

The old woman grumbled and snatched up a shortcake biscuit. She dipped it in her tea and ate half. "Not for the better."

"If you're so averse to the Internet," said Ed. "How did you find out this was happening?"

"One of the girls at my bingo set the app up for me on my phone so I could watch cooking videos. I like to try new recipes, you see? Not much else to enjoy at my age." She flexed her hands out in front of her, suggesting she had arthritis. "Anyway, the novelty wore off, but for a while I used the app quite a lot. The church where I grew up also started posting live sermons, which really brought me back to my youth. Have you ever praised the Lord in Italian? I swear it brings you much closer to Him than English does."

"I'll take your word for it," said Shane, having been an atheist ever since... He cleared his throat. "So you've been using the app for a while? How did you find out about the ritual?"

Gina ate the second half of her biscuit, making them wait while she chewed slowly. After she swallowed, she picked up her tea and took a swig. Eventually, she got around to answering his question. "Must have been that – what do you call it? – algorithm. The app used to send me daily prayers and sermons, things like that. It must've thought the ritual was something I'd be interested in." She did the sign of the cross. "Blasted thing."

"We haven't got around to translating the ritual yet," said Ed. "Do you know what the words mean? They're Latin, right?"

"Yes, dear. I know the words all right, but until this week, I hadn't heard them spoken since I was a very young girl." She took a deep breath. "With the name of the secret you hid from the door, I report to my lost friend from the fall. Keep safe all those who beseech the lost. Revive the soul at night. Revive the soul at night. Revive the soul at night. Amen."

Shane frowned. It wasn't as foreboding as he'd assumed, but perhaps English was more benign than Latin. "Do you believe in the ritual?"

"It's as real as the air we're breathing." She took another swig of tea and then licked the thin membrane of her lips. "And more dangerous than you know."

"Then why on earth would you speak it out loud?" He looked around, feigning anxiety, fighting the urge to ridicule her but failing in his tone. "Is a ghost going to appear and murder us all? Who is it? Anyone we know? Maybe it's Churchill."

"Are you mocking me, Mr Mogg?"

"If you believe in the words, then why would you say them?"

"Because they have to be spoken in Latin. The Lord doesn't recognise English. It doesn't hold power like the ancient languages. Syrian, Greek, Hebrew, Latin... those are the tongues that stir Heaven."

Shane couldn't help it. He rolled his eyes. "Convenient. Okay, so why would someone release the ritual – in Latin – on the Internet?"

"How should I know? That's why I contacted a journalist. It's your job to figure things out, right? Whoever did it must have their reasons, but they're undeniably wicked.

Tormenting the dead at the expense of the innocent..." She shook her head in disgust. "It's just evil."

"Maybe it was you," said Shane. He still had an unshakeable feeling that this was all some big prank. Maybe he was being targeted for some unknown offence. Had he cut someone up on the highway? Sworn at a telemarketer in a drunken stupor? Written an unflattering article about someone?

There was that time I said Ariana Grande was really a forty-year-old woman masquerading as a child star, but I was clearly joking.

Gina shook her head wearily. "Is that the best you've got? Accusing an old woman who's just trying to help? God save those poor children."

"Yes, let's pray they aren't devoured by legions of the dead,"

Ed grunted. "You're being an arse, Shane. Pack it in."

"Sorry. I just... I just find this all very hard to believe."

"It's time you started to believe, Mr Mogg. For we walk by faith, not by sight."

Shane rolled his eyes. "Two Corinthians. 5:7."

Gina flinched. "You know your Bible?"

"Every damned page, and if it taught me anything, it's that people are too eager to live their lives by rules and laws set by men long since dead."

"Perhaps you're right. I've always thought the biggest problem with Christianity is the men running it. That's why I left the convent all the way back in nineteen seventy-two."

Shane's legs ached, so he finally gave in and pulled up a

chair. He sat to the side of Gina, with Ed just over his shoulder at the edge of the room. "You were a nun?"

"*Si!* A sister of the Holy Mountain in Maletto from the age of nineteen to twenty-four. I was a poor girl in a poor village, so the Church was a chance to escape poverty and hardship. Little did I know I would be serving the abbot and his monks far more than I served the Lord. Just another woman forced into quiet obedience. Perhaps, if I'd remained that way, I never would have learned of Nomon's Ritual."

"So how did you?" Shane was surprised to find a begrudging respect for this woman now. He was no fan of the Church either, and her criticism of it warmed him to her. It couldn't have been easy for a woman in those days to defy authority.

"I used to creep around at night," she said. "Usually to sneak books from the library or wine from the cellars. The monks did as they pleased, so why shouldn't I?" She smiled and looked off to the side, as if remembering her youthful self fondly. "I suppose I liked the danger of getting caught. Anyhow, that's beside the point. One night, I discovered several of the brothers gathered in a chamber off the back of the library. Being nosey by nature, I wanted to know what they were up to, so I climbed up the bookshelves and into the rafters, where I could see them but they couldn't see me. Till the day I die, I'll always remember the first time I saw the ritual performed."

"Wait," said Ed. "So the ritual is... holy? It's part of the Church?"

"Oh, yes. Summoning the dead used to be a regular practice, although one shrouded in secrecy. Our monastery was the only place permitted to perform the ritual in all of Sicily."

"But why would the Church want to summon the dead?" Shane tried to suppress his incredulity, wary of upsetting Ed again. She was still glaring at him from the side of the room.

Gina shook her head at him as if he were a fool. "What's the best way to find out about the past, or discover the person responsible for a murder? You ask those who were there."

"Wow," said Ed, leaning forward and propping her chin against her palm. "That's just... wow."

Gina smiled at her. "Your hair is lovely, miss. I've been meaning to say. Pink! What confidence."

Ed blushed. "Um, thanks."

"It is 'miss', right? I should've checked. I don't mind calling you a them or a whatsit."

Ed's blushes turned to chuckles. "I'm a gay woman, but you can call me whatever you like. Maybe go with Ed?"

"It's lovely to meet you, Ed."

"Likewise."

"Tell us about the ritual," said Shane impatiently. "Everything you know."

"Okay, okay. Well, the first time I saw it, the abbot and his senior monks were bringing back a poor soul by the name of Leonardo Verga. Leonardo had died decades before during the Second World War, fighting for Mussolini's fascists. The Church wanted to locate a holy relic stolen by the blackshirts, and they believed this poor dead soldier might know where it was. Turns out they were right. He'd buried it off in some field."

Shane raised an eyebrow at her. "They brought him back... and he answered?"

"Not willingly, but yes. They performed the ritual, and Leonardo appeared inside a circle of candles they'd set up. Screeched and spat like a cornered cat, he did, and the darkness of his sins billowed off him like smoke, coating the stone walls in ash. It caused the brothers no small amount of coughing and spluttering, but they persisted. Each of them detested the dead and took great pleasure in tormenting Leonardo Verga. He snatched and clawed at them but could not leave the candles. A circle is a powerful symbol, you see? Unbroken, unbent, and without end – like the majesty of our Lord."

"Hold on," said Shane, rubbing at the stubble on his chin. "If I accept that the ritual is real, then these kids are getting hurt because the dead are attacking them, right? Is it because they're not lighting candles?"

Gina shook her head, and for a moment she seemed older – a weak old lady looking very sad. "The candles are just an added protection," she said. "It's the binding words that keep the dead contained. 'Keep safe all those who beseech the lost.' It implores the fallen one to keep those who perform the ritual from harm."

"Fallen one?" Shane looked her in the eye. "You mean Lucifer?"

Gina did the sign of the cross. "Speak not his name, lest his focus falls upon you."

Ed cleared her throat and shuffled her seat over to the table to join them properly. "Gina? Why did Stefani and Hannah get hurt but not the monks?"

"Because they didn't speak all the words of the ritual.

They left out the plea of binding. Whoever originally posted it online must have omitted that part. Without it, the dead are returned without shackles to do as they please."

Ed groaned. Clearly, she believed Gina's story, or was at least enthralled enough by it to forget that she didn't. Shane was still far from convinced though. Religious mumbo jumbo was something with which he had great experience, despite severing its hold on his life many years ago.

When I learned God didn't exist.

But, whether he believed in Gina's story or not, he was deep in this now. The story was incomplete. He couldn't stop until he had all the answers.

And it's not like I have anything better to do.

"I found the original poster," he said. "Someone named Vita."

Gina's eyes lit up and some of the signs of age went away. She must have been at least seventy, but right then she became vital and alert. "Life," she said.

Shane frowned. "Huh?"

"Vita. It means 'Life' in Italian. Show me. Show me what you've found."

"Okay." Shane got up with a sigh. "Let me go fetch my laptop."

Shane showed the video to Gina and Ed. Neither had much to say, but both asked him to play it a second time and then a third. Afterwards, they sat in thoughtful silence, with Gina clutching her glittery cross and Ed chewing her black-painted fingernails. Meanwhile, Shane checked Clip

Switch on his phone. The ritual was still viral, with dozens of new videos being posted every hour. News was finally trickling through on the web, but it was questionable. More drug overdoses, tragic mishaps, and suicide pacts. None of the articles mentioned ghosts, or even the ritual in most cases. If they reported on ghostly murders, they could get sued left, right, and centre for being irresponsible and offensive. If they wrote about it speculatively, they would be mocked. Worst of all, if they dared to take it seriously, they might incite a nationwide panic.

When Shane started seeing videos from Canada and America, he realised that thinking nationwide was narrow-minded.

Kids are doing this all over the world.

Maybe someone in the States will expose what's going on. They can call it Ritualgate and unveil a cabal of Midwestern satanists behind it. Let it be a cult of serial killers or a mass suicide pact. Just not ghosts.

Several of the videos had been taken down or placed under review. Clip Switch clearly knew something was going on.

Gina kept glancing at Shane periodically, as if she wanted to say something but was unsure whether to or not. Eventually, it irritated him enough that he asked her what was wrong.

"Oh, it might be nothing," she said. "It's about the video."

"Okay. What is it?"

"It's difficult to tell, because Vita was speaking Latin, but I swear I could detect an accent. It reminded me of home."

He frowned at her. "Of Sicily?"

Gina nodded. "The way he spoke the words, especially the *amen* at the end. Then there's his name, Vita. He could be Italian. I might be wrong."

Shane nodded to himself, giving it some thought. "No, that's helpful, thank you. Maybe if you watch it again, you can—"

Rachel entered the conference room then, startling them all. She looked at Shane, at Ed, and then finally at Gina. "Um... hello?" she said.

Shane slid his phone into his pocket as if she'd caught him watching porn. "R-Rachel? What are you doing here?"

"Oh my God, I'm sorry. I forgot my laptop charger. I-I'm working from home tomorrow because I have to watch my sister's kid and—"

Shane nodded. "No problem. Go ahead and get it."

"I will. Um, why are you here so late? It's half past seven."

He nodded at Gina, who waved a frail, tissue-paper hand at Rachel. "I had a late interview walk in."

"Oh, are you still looking into that ritual on Clip Switch?"

Shane gasped. "How do you know what I'm working on?"

"I'm in charge of the website and server. Someone tried to send you an email, but they mistyped your address so it redirected to the system inbox. I forwarded it on to you this morning."

Gina rubbed at her knuckles and chuckled. "Arthritis. My typing is awful."

Shane marched over to his laptop and pulled up Gina's

original email. Sure enough, there was a bunch of metadata he'd missed. The email had come via *Splatt!*'s default inbox, not directly from Gina, because she'd spelled his name in the address as *Shne*. "Oh. I didn't know that was a thing that happened."

"Only sometimes," said Rachel. "I didn't mean to read it, but it caught my interest, so I looked up the ritual online. It's horrible. Are kids really getting hurt by... by ghosts?"

She seemed genuinely upset, maybe even a little afraid. Rachel was a sweet girl, if a little dim-witted, yet he hadn't known she was so empathetic that she would get teary-eyed about a bunch of random teenagers.

Ed cleared her throat and caught Shane's eye, seeming to indicate that he should do something.

Does she want me to go give Rachel a hug, or throw her out? Could be either.

Rachel clutched at her chest. "I get so easily disturbed. When I was thirteen, I stayed at a friend's house, and we saw a ghost at the bottom of the stairs at midnight. Scares the heck out of me to this day."

"It's, um, okay," said Shane, fighting the urge to ridicule her story. "It's all just a big online prank. That's what my story is going to be about. I'm trying to find the people responsible. Hey, do you want to help?"

She raised her head and looked at him. "How?"

"Go home and rest, because tomorrow I want you to work on a side column for me about the effects of video trends on today's youth. I want the good, the bad, and the questionable. Keep it to about two thousand words."

She gasped. "You want me to write an article all by myself?"

"Think you're ready?"

"Yes! I would really like to try."

He gave her the biggest smile he could manage. "Time to put that Media Studies A level to use, huh?"

She leapt forward and hugged him. "Thank you so much, Shane. You won't regret this."

He stiffened up and eased her back. "Yeah, um, no problem. You deserve it. Now go home and get some rest, okay?"

She nodded repeatedly. "I'll just grab my charger and then I'll get out of your hair. I'm so excited!"

Shane stood still, watching her rush about, not wanting to resume his investigation until she'd left the building. Once she had, he let out a sigh. "Jesus, I thought she was going to have a breakdown. What was that?"

"She lost her dad a few months back," said Ed. "You should have comforted her. She wanted you to. I think she has a thing for you."

"What? I'm twice her age."

"You don't have to marry her, but a fling never hurt anybody."

"Amen," said Gina with a wink.

"That literally isn't true," said Shane. "Anyway, I *did* comfort her."

Ed nodded. "I guess you did. It was nice of you. Why did you give her an article?"

"The magazine is going bust. She should get a chance to put something worthwhile on her resume. We owe her that much."

"No," said Ed, with an infuriating chuckle. "It's more

than that. Shane Mogg, you were just kind to another human being for no reason."

"I just wanted to occupy her mind so she wouldn't fixate on this grisly business of ours. She's too sensitive." He decided that was harsh and corrected himself. "I didn't know her dad died recently. That sucks."

"Everyone else in the office knew about it," said Ed. "You should pay more attention."

Shane didn't like the way the conversation was making him feel – guilty – so he changed the subject. "Any idea how we can track down this Vita?"

"No," said Ed. "But I have a question for Gina that I'm hoping she'll know the answer to."

Gina sipped her tea. "Ask away."

"Why do some ghosts attack and others don't?"

"I wondered that myself," said Shane. "A bit inconsistent, isn't it?"

Gina frowned. "I'm sorry, what do you mean?"

"Stefani and Hannah were attacked immediately after performing the ritual," said Ed, "and so were Jenna and Finn. We met a girl, though, who wasn't attacked. Her grandmother visited her after she performed the ritual but did nothing to hurt her. In fact, she woke up to find her dead grandma stroking her hair."

"I guess ghosts are like people," said Shane. "Some are just dicks."

Gina scrunched up her face at him, her wrinkles becoming deep creases. "You should take this seriously, Mr Mogg. As for your question, Ed, I don't know the answer. But I do know that the dead are never happy to be brought back. They are twisted by the barbarity of Hell, or bereaved at having been ripped away from Heaven. If this grandmother has not yet attacked, I can only imagine it's because a part of who she once was still exists. Eventually, I fear she'll grow too weak to resist the rage inside her."

"Wait," said Ed. "So you think this girl is in danger?"

"Possibly. Probably. But so are many others. We can't help them one by one. We need to end this thing completely by finding out who Vita is and figuring out a way to stop this thing from spreading any further."

"I agree about finding Vita," said Shane. "He's the key to all this."

"I agree too," said Ed. "But what about the kids who have already performed the ritual? What can we do to help them?"

Gina put her hands around her mug and stared into it with a long, drawn-out sigh. "We pray for their souls, dear."

"Great," said Shane. "That'll fix things."

Gina glared at him, but he didn't care.

CHAPTER EIGHT

They ordered pizza, which arrived at eight fifteen. It was now pitch-black outside the office, the nearest light source coming from the McDonald's across the road. Charges on the company credit card always got flagged up on Bernard's phone, so to pre-empt a call, Shane sent his boss a text explaining that he and Ed had returned to the office to work on something. Bernard had taken some convincing, seeing as Shane hadn't worked late once in the last three years, but a second text from Ed had eventually put his worries to bed.

Gina was unimpressed by the margarita-stuffed crust, but she forced down two slices anyway. As a native Sicilian, she probably had strong opinions about pizza.

Shane was finishing up his fourth slice, yawning between each mouthful. It'd been a long day, and he would soon have no choice but to halt things until tomorrow morning when they could start again. Too late to chase leads now; all they could do was research and the collation of facts. Ed was looking into the Vita video, and she had sent the link to a videographer she'd recently worked with at *Country Home* magazine. She claimed the guy would be able to enhance the audio and maybe find out for certain what words the robed stranger was mumbling.

That had been ten minutes ago though. Now Ed was talking on her mobile phone in the corner of the conference room, but she didn't seem to be following up on work. It seemed like a personal call. A bad one.

Is someone shouting down the line at her? She looks angry. No... she looks upset.

What's going on?

Needing a brief mental pause from dying teenagers and occult rituals, Shane stood by and waited for Ed to finish her call. Once she had, he approached her. "Everything all right?"

For a moment, she didn't meet his eyeline, just stared at the carpet and breathed heavily. He considered reaching out and touching her, but didn't want it to be misconstrued. So he waited until she was ready to look at him. "My landlord's being a prick," she eventually said. "He's sticking the rent up on my flat by thirty per cent."

"Can he do that?"

"Probably. The thing is, he doesn't even want me as a tenant. I have a friend who's an estate agent, and she reckons he wants to divide the flat and rent it out as two separate units. I've already met his last two increases, but it's clear he'll keep doing it until I leave."

Shane folded his arms and tutted. He had opinions about people owning property solely to rent out. People having a place to live shouldn't be a business. "You need to talk to Bernard," he said. "I think he rents a place out on the coast. He might know what your rights are."

"He has a holiday home. It's not the same. Anyway, I don't want to live in a place where I know the owner wants me gone. I'm not one of those people who picks a fight out of principle. Just give me a quiet life."

"What are you going to do?"

"Find some other place to live, I suppose." She shook her head and sighed. "Wish I'd bought a place like you, back when it was just about affordable. What do you have, three bedrooms? A garden?"

He nodded but got the sense he was being attacked. Was she mad that he owned a house? She probably earned more than he did, so it was hardly his fault. Perhaps he was missing something. "If you need help moving, my Land Cruiser is all yours."

"Gee, thanks. You're such a good friend."

He frowned, taken aback by her tone. Before he could ask what was wrong, she dodged by him and stormed out of the conference room, probably to go get some air. Hopefully, when she returned, she would explain why she was mad at him.

She's mad at her landlord and just taking it out on me. One of the many benefits of friendship.

Shane went and checked on Gina, who looked ready to nod off. She wasn't exactly savvy with computers, so was mainly there to act as a reference for Ed and Shane whenever they found something useful to run by her.

After Gina assured him she was fine, he went to make himself a coffee. Usually, he would be on his second beer by now, slumped in front of Netflix, or one of the other streaming services – legal or illegal – he made nightly use of. Lately, he'd been watching the *Lord of the Rings* films, enjoying the nostalgia of having watched them at the cinema as a teen – when life had been rosier. In fact, he remembered going on a first date there, although that memory was bittersweet. All memories of Emily were.

Hard to believe he was thirty-nine. Even more surprising that he was still relatively healthy and in shape. By all rights, he should have a beer gut and gout, but he had somehow avoided both. Further proof, in his mind, that having kids aged the shit out of you.

At least, having kids that don't die before you even get to know them.

The coffee machine sputtered and spat scalding water onto his hand, which did nothing to help his mood. Ed's snappiness had irritated him, but he knew it was really the hankering for alcohol that was gradually eroding his temper. His patience had been thinning since first interviewing Gina. Now he was seething that his hand was burned.

"Stupid bloody thing," he said, and he bashed the machine on its side, causing coffee to spill out of his mug and into the drip tray. Fortunately, when he brought it to his lips, it tasted good and was exactly what he needed. Tea or coffee, there was just something about a hot drink that brought down the pressure. No one ever flew off the handle with a cup of hot tea in their hand.

Okay, just relax. It's been a tough day, but no one here is to blame. Let's not be any more misanthropic than usual.

Gina remained sitting in the conference room. She had pulled a sudoku book from her giant tote bag and was now jotting in it with a small blue pen. Shane had never seen the appeal himself. He'd always been more of an arrow word kind of guy.

His hand smarted and was beginning to turn red – best he get some cold water on it – so he put down his coffee on one of the desks in the open-plan area of the office and headed for the toilets in the entrance corridor.

The men's room wasn't luxurious by any length of the imagination – just a pair of urinals with rusting pipework and a single water closet opposite two sinks – but at least it got cleaned every morning by an agency worker. A single sheet of long glass ran behind the wall-mounted sinks, four feet wide by three feet high. The steel taps were old – and a pain to turn on when they were cold – but not so old that they were worth paying to replace. There was barely enough budget to buy toilet paper each month.

Shane went over to a sink on the left and wrenched the cold tap until it was fully open. The rushing water was icy cold but increased to tepid within a few seconds. He held his scalded hand beneath the stream and winced at the tingling pain.

A loud clunk sounded, and the taps started to rattle, as did the pipes below the sinks. The gushing water sputtered and then stopped altogether. Shane fiddled with the handles, wrenching them back and forth, but the water didn't return. His hand glistened with moisture, but his scald had already come out in a red, ragged blotch. A shitty end to a shitty day.

He stared at himself in the mirror and reminded himself he was still sane. "You can get to the bottom of this. You can figure it out. Those kids got hurt for a reason, and for once in your life you're going to act like a proper journalist and find answers." He rubbed at his face, stretching out his eyelids and groaning at the sight of himself. For a moment, he saw a semblance of his mother in the narrow bridge of his nose, but the rest of him was his father – a man who had died driving a bus at fifty-two while Shane had been only six. One of Shane's biggest fears was that he had his father's weak heart – a ticking time bomb in his chest – but he had never had it checked. It made the future blurry and unpromised.

He closed his eyes and tried to listen to his heartbeat, tried to feel his pulse thrumming in his temples, and reassure himself he was still alive. Not dead. Not a ghost.

Because ghosts don't exist.

And yet he drifted through life just like one. Sure, he lived by his own rules, without pressure, but would he one day reach a point where he realised he had got it all wrong? And by then, would it be too late to course-correct?

"Everything's fine," he told himself, and then he opened his eyes.

He didn't expect to see his daughter.

But Mandy was staring right at him.

Shane's dead daughter peered up at the mirror from behind him. Her skin was the colour and texture of porcelain, her dark brown hair frizzy and unkempt, but it was definitely her – looking at him with those innocent brown eyes he'd fallen in love with the moment she'd been born.

Shane's hands gripped the sink like a pair of claws. His knees locked in place like crooked pinions. He tried to close his eyes again but couldn't. If he did, Mandy might disappear, and he didn't want her to go. Yet seeing her in the mirror chilled his blood.

She's really there, standing right behind me. I'm looking at my dead daughter.

It took everything he had to turn his head.

He expected to see nothing but empty floor tiles.

But he was wrong.

Mandy peered up at him, unsteady on her chubby two-year-old legs. Those deep brown eyes locked onto his. Something about them was wrong. Her eyes were empty.

"Dah."

"Mandy?" Shane couldn't help himself. He reached out to his daughter.

With a feral shriek, she clawed at the exposed flesh of his wrist.

Suddenly, he was bleeding. He reeled backwards, striking his hip against the sink and adding a rattling bone ache to the white-hot flare of his slashed wrist. His dead daughter had just attacked him. This was real.

But impossible.

"M-Mandy? It's okay. Sweetie, it's okay."

She glared at him like a rabid dog. Shane didn't know what to do. Should he grab her and wrestle her, or should he get the hell out of there? Was any part of his daughter truly here in this bathroom with him? Could she hear his words? Understand them?

Was this a chance for him to say goodbye?

He lowered into a crouch, matching Mandy's height, and put out a trembling hand as a protective barrier between them. "The night you died, I died."

Mandy took a step towards him. Her dark hair had

been so thick and lustrous in life, always prompting comments from broody strangers, but it was lank now and devoid of nourishment. Her skin lacked life, pale and sickly.

My little girl is dead.

But she's still my little girl.

"Mandy, I'm so sorry. I would give my life if I could—"

"*Abba!*" Mandy threw herself at Shane, clawing at his face and snapping her tiny jaws at him. The odour that escaped her was worse than death. It was beyond death.

Damnation.

No. Not my little girl.

Shane did everything he could to cover himself, but he was knocked sprawling onto the tiles. Mandy clung to him, mauled him, and bit into his flailing arms with jagged teeth.

His mind finally snapped.

His entire soul screamed to the tune of torment.

Shane curled into a ball, his body crying out from repeated blows and slashes. He felt patches of acute burning along with spreading cold aches as his pain receptors were overwhelmed. He knew he was screaming, but it felt distant, coming from a place far away. In fact, his entire body felt detached from his shattered mind.

He was only vaguely aware of someone else being in the room.

"Mr Mogg? What on earth has happened?"

"Please make her stop. Make her stop!"

"Who? What are you talking about? Mr Mogg? You're bleeding!"

Shane lay still, waiting for the next bout of agony, but nothing came. Slowly, he opened his eyes and found himself staring at the cracked paintwork on the walls. The voice had come from behind him. "G-Gina, is that you?"

"Yes, it's me." She sounded panicked. "Do you need me to call someone? What happened to you?"

He rolled over to face her, glancing around the toilets in disbelief. The room was empty except for them. His daughter was gone. Or had never been there at all.

"M-Mandy."

Gina shook her head at him. "What happened? Why are you covered in blood?"

Shane examined himself and saw gashes on his arms, slices on his hands. There was no way he'd imagined it. This was no mental breakdown or stress-induced hallucination. He'd been attacked by… by something.

"M-my daughter. She was here."

Gina put a hand on the nearest sink to take some of her weight. She was breathing heavily. "Y-your daughter? I don't understand."

"She attacked me. My daughter attacked me. But-but it's not possible. Mandy's dead. She died over ten years ago. At two years old."

Gina wavered unsteadily. "How can that be, Mr Mogg?"

"Because…" He shook his head. "Because I performed the ritual."

"Oh, momma mia, you foolish man." She put a trembling hand to her head and winced.

Shane sat up and wrapped his arms around his knees like a child. He rocked back and forth, and although he tried to fight it, he broke down sobbing.

"Okay. Okay…" Gina reached out a frail hand and

gently touched the top of Shane's head. "Let's get you off this dirty floor. You're safe now. It's over."

He looked up at her, his vision blurry. "You don't know that. What if she comes back?"

"Then next time you won't be alone. I'll stay with you."

He chuckled, embarrassed to actually find comfort in the guardianship of a seventy-year-old woman. It gave him enough of a boost to drag himself up off the floor. Everything hurt, and droplets of his blood shone on the tiles as he rose, groaning, to his feet.

Gina reached out and squeezed his shoulder. "Easy there. I'm not strong enough to catch you."

He tested his balance, taking a step to the side and then back again. "I think I'm okay. Where's Ed?"

"She left."

"What?" He looked past her shoulder at the door. "Why?"

"I don't know. She never came back after her phone call. I heard a car outside leaving."

He shook his head, wondering why Ed would leave without saying anything. She was clearly pissed off about something, but he couldn't imagine it was down to him. Was it her landlord?

Gina eased him towards the door. "Let's get you a cuppa. I could certainly use one. Your screaming gave me the fright of my life."

"I already made a coffee," he said vacantly. "I burned myself."

"Oh dear. Never mind. Come on now."

He nodded and allowed her to lead him back inside the conference room. She then went to make him a cup of tea in the tiny kitchenette beside Bernard's office, after warning him he should avoid too much caffeine at night. He almost followed her, not wanting to be alone, but he consoled himself with the fact she would remain within shouting distance. While he waited, he tried calling Ed, but her phone went straight to voicemail. He couldn't cope with worrying about her right now, so he attempted to clear his mind of everything.

A field of green grass. A gently rolling sea. Beano comics under my bed as a kid. Nice things. Calm things.

Gina returned five minutes later with two steaming mugs of tea. She sat down next to Shane and set both drinks down on the pine desk. Bernard would be livid if he knew they weren't using coasters, but Shane couldn't bring himself to care about such trivial things.

"It was my daughter," he said. "It was her."

Gina nodded, no sign of argument. "Are you okay?"

"No! Not even close. How is this possible?"

"I don't know, Mr Mogg. It just is. I'm sorry."

He shook his head and stared into his tea, the condensation collecting against his forehead. "Why would she attack me? I loved Mandy. I did everything a father was supposed to do."

"The dead are just echoes of who they once were. Your daughter's soul was probably in Heaven, but now she's back here, in this place, where pain and suffering exist again. It must be like getting woken from a wonderful dream by a terrible, unrelenting din. You would lash out instinctively, I suppose."

"Mandy's suffering?"

Gina sighed. "I would love to lie to you, Mr Mogg, but

the dead don't return to soothe us and give us peace. Your daughter, like all the others brought back because of this wretched ritual, has been dragged here against her will. All she must feel is anger. Confusion, at the very least."

Tears spilled from Shane's eyes, stinging the scratches on his cheeks. His teeth locked together, and he struggled to part them. "Y-you were a nun?"

"A lifetime ago."

He didn't mean to, but he snarled at her. "How can you believe in a god that would make this possible? My daughter is innocent. Just like she was innocent when God took her and her mother away from me."

Gina looked at him, her eyes rheumy yet wise. As she exhaled, she asked him what happened. "Share your pain with me. Talk it out."

"I can't share it. It's mine."

"Well, tell me anyway, dear."

He shook his head and looked away. "What is there to tell? I grew up being a good little Christian boy – did exactly what my mother told me. Went to church three times a week, never swore, never took the Lord's name in vain, and I certainly never spent any time with the opposite sex. Ha! If I even so much as thought about girls in that way, I would beat myself up for days afterwards." He huffed, feeling the spite rise inside of him. "I never even dared masturbate till I was seventeen, in case I damned my soul to Hell. I wept afterwards."

Gina grimaced, but she didn't interrupt him.

So he went on. "One time, when I was about nine or ten, I argued with my mother about God. I'd been learning about other religions at school, and I became convinced there were lots of different gods in Heaven. It just made sense to me. My mum didn't appreciate my new beliefs though, so she poured a bag of dried rice on the floor and had me kneel on it for hours while I prayed. You know, sometimes, when it's cold, my knees still ache from it." He sighed. "I don't know, maybe the pain's just in my head."

"I'm sorry," said Gina, swallowing, and licking at her thin gossamer lips. "Your mother had no right to punish you for childhood curiosity."

He shrugged. "It doesn't matter. The only reason I'm telling you this is so you know I did everything I was supposed to do. I fell in love, married a girl from my church, and then we had a child. That's how you honour God, right? Raise a family, teach them the Bible, repeat the cycle?"

"I believe family is God's true Church."

He rose in his seat, fists clenched on top of his knees. "Then why the fuck did God take them from me? I did everything I could to please the holy fucking Lord. Emily and Mandy were innocent. Why did He take them?"

"I don't know."

"He moves in mysterious ways, right? Isn't that the company line for questions that can't be answered?"

Gina shrugged, offering him the slightest of smiles. "I understand your anger, Mr Mogg. I lost a child too."

"Y-you did?"

She shrugged. "So long ago now, but the pain is still with me. My David and I tried for a family several times. I had two miscarriages first, but eventually I had a pregnancy that took. Unfortunately, that one ended up stillborn. We named her Marie and had a little funeral for her. After that, we never wanted to try again. For whatever reason, David and I were never supposed to be parents."

Shane couldn't look her in the eye. He didn't know who had suffered worse. He and Emily had had two years with Mandy, but that made the loss hurt even worse.

But would I give up those two years?

"I'm sorry, Gina. It's not every day I meet someone who's had a shittier life than me."

"I've had a wonderful life," she said. "But part of life is being in pain. It's unavoidable."

"That doesn't make it any easier."

"How did they die? Your family?"

It surprised him that she dared ask. His anger must have been clear on his face, yet she prodded him instead of appeased him. "A car crash," he said. "What a cliche, huh? Emily was driving over a bridge, coming back from the supermarket with Mandy in the back of the car, when a bunch of joyriding kids swerved across the road. She had to steer to avoid them. Car flipped over the barricade and into the River Peck below. They drowned with their seatbelts on. Safety first, right?"

A tear spilled from Gina's eye. The sight of it shocked Shane, filling him with a furious rage, but also a desperate sadness. It was his pain, and she had no right to feel it, and yet...

"It's not your fault," he said, lifting his hands and warming them around his mug. "Just how it is. Things happen in a godless world."

She reached out and placed a hand on his wrist. Her fingers were ice cold. "This isn't a godless world, Mr Mogg. Has today not shown you that?"

"God didn't bring back the dead. It's the other guy, right? The Devil?"

She did the sign of the cross but didn't cease looking him in the eye. "You can't have one without the other. Joy only exists in the absence of pain. God is the same way. Perhaps it was his counterpart who took your family from you. Maybe God had nothing to do with it. You wanted to believe once that there were multiple forces in Heaven. Perhaps you were right."

"Wouldn't that make God a bit useless?"

"Or maybe God can only do so much, like any of us. Perhaps He has regrets of His own."

Shane rubbed his face, spreading the warmth from his palms. He felt drunk, despite not having had a drop in over twenty-four hours. "This is real, isn't it? I mean, ghosts *are* attacking people. My daughter came back from the dead to hurt me."

Gina sighed. "It's real, Mr Mogg, and we need to stop it. Every naïve young fool who did the ritual is now in danger. If they haven't been attacked already, they will be soon. And it won't stop until they're dead."

Shane nodded. He finally understood.

That nothing made sense.

CHAPTER NINE

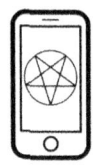

"I'm sorry for doubting you," Shane told Gina as they sipped their tea. He wasn't sure what to do next. How exactly were you meant to function after experiencing something like what had just happened to him? As well as being mentally obliterated, he was also bleeding from a dozen shallow cuts. His hip was bruised from bashing against the sink. The pain made it hard to think.

All he knew was that he didn't want to be alone. Nor did he want to fully contemplate what had just happened. He needed to distract himself, or he would lose what was left of his mind. It was all he could do just to keep from quivering like a jelly, and he had to clutch both hands in his lap to keep them still. If he had been a smoker, now would have been the moment to light up.

"It's okay," she said. "I suppose this entire thing is hard to believe. The girls at bingo would have me sectioned if they knew I was here with you now, trying to stop a bunch of ghosts."

Shane chuckled, making a sound that was brittle and

on edge. "I'm glad you're here. You're a fount of knowledge."

"I'm just old."

"Hey, not many people your age are on Clip Switch. Even less willing to do what you're doing now."

"It's nice to be useful. Older I get, the more it feels like the world has little need of me. It's felt that way since my David died."

"Tell me about him. You said he was an opera singer?"

Just talk to me and keep me calm. Please!

"He was a tenor. My David could reach right inside you with his voice. Like a force of nature, he was. Sometimes, I sit and listen to his old CDs and it's like he never left."

"He must have been very talented. How did you meet?"

"He was touring Europe with a ballet company. I had left Sicily by then and was living in Turin, working as a cleaner at a little theatre named *La Scintilla*. David was performing there for two weeks, and during that time I often tidied up his dressing room. Most performers looked down their noses at theatre staff, but David was different. He was this warm, loving man who showed an interest in everyone around him." She winked. "But me most of all."

Shane smiled. "I bet you were a looker."

"More than I am now, that's for sure. Anyway, David spoke a little Italian thanks to his years studying and performing opera, so we got to chatting. This was his third tour of the country, and he always loved visiting, but he wanted to see more than just the same old tourist spots. So I offered to show him parts of the city he'd never been to, like the *Palazzo Falletti di Barolo* and the *Colline del Po*. The real Turin. By the end of the week, we couldn't bear to be apart, and I accompanied him for the rest of his European tour. When it ended six months later in Monte Carlo, David took me home to Cardiff and married me."

"Wow. Didn't you miss home?"

"Every day, but I would've missed David more. Anyway, he toured Italy six more times in our years together, so I had plenty of chances to go home. It never felt out of reach. As for family" – she shrugged – "I had none. My father died in the early days of the Second World War and my mother died while I was in the convent. By the time I left Italy, I had no one."

Shane folded his hands in his lap, wondering what such a life would be like. To follow love across borders, to throw caution to the wind. To live by the whims of one's heartstrings. "Why did you leave the convent? You never said."

"Lust."

"Wait, you didn't fool around at the monastery, did you?"

Gina smiled, a twinkle in her eye. For a moment, she seemed twenty years younger. "Brother Antonio. A Venetian rogue who came late to God's grace. He was a novice, yet well into his thirties after a lifetime of drifting from one place to another, working odd jobs and joining the crews of various merchant ships. He'd travelled the entire Mediterranean by the time he came to us. Oh, the stories he could tell. And his body..." She grinned. "Hardened by a life of adventure."

Amused, Shane said, "I'm assuming romantic affairs were banned in the monastery?"

"Absolutely forbidden. But even servants of God are human, and humans are built a certain way. After a year of midnight meet-ups and secret dalliances, the abbot finally caught Antonio and I canoodling in the chapter house. He had walked in with the town mayor, about to hold a meeting, but he found us both naked beneath the table. Humiliated isn't even the word for it. I've never seen a man turn so red."

Shane cringed as he imagined the panic she must have felt. "So what happened?"

"What do you think? The abbot branded me a harlot for tempting Brother Antonio."

"Were you punished?"

"Of course. Antonio was given a month of the lowliest duties as punishment for his weakness, but I was whipped bloody and given a six-month vow of silence. Every monk in the monastery was told to avert their gaze in my presence until my penance was over. The worst part was that even Brother Antonio ignored me after that, as if he hadn't professed his love to me a hundred times before."

Shane sneered. "Bastard."

"Calm down, dear. I survived, didn't I? In fact, it was only a week later I absconded under the cover of darkness on a path that would eventually lead me to find my David. If they'd caught me, there would've been hell to pay, but I convinced a local boat captain to take me to Capua on the mainland. He thought having a nun onboard would bring him good luck." She picked up her mug and took a sip of tea. "I never went back to Sicily ever again, but I often think about Antonio. He'd be an old man now, if he still lives. Eighty, I'd say." She let out a sigh and laced her gnarled fingers together on the table. "After my David died, I thought about tracking him down – to tell him what a wonderful life I've lived, and how I came far closer to God than I ever would have within the walls of that wretched monastery." She turned slightly in her seat and lifted her blouse. Scars crisscrossed the pale flesh of her back. "This isn't God's work."

Shane swore. The world often felt like a rotten place, so it was easy to forget that there had once been a time when things had been even worse. To whip a woman like Gina for daring to love a man... "I'm sorry that happened to you. I'm surprised you kept your faith."

"Why would I blame God for the actions of men? The Lord kept me safe and allowed me to escape to the mainland so that I could one day find real love. Hardships are necessary to appreciate the good things in our lives." She grabbed the glittery cross on her breast. "For instance, I robbed this from the abbot's secret stash before I did a midnight flit. Thing's probably worth a fortune."

Shane cackled so loud he made himself flinch, but it was short-lived as his mind quickly returned to reality and moved away from thieving nuns and their illicit love affairs. "What if you have no good things in your life?"

"Oh, Mr Mogg, you are a negative Nelly, aren't you? You're a talented, compassionate individual."

"Not sure compassionate is a word people would use to describe me."

"I contacted a dozen different people to help me, but you're the only one who gave me the time of day."

"Because I wanted a story, not to help you."

"And yet here we are, trying to put a stop to this. You

and Ed have run yourselves ragged today. It hasn't all been about getting a story."

Shane shifted awkwardly in his seat, hands around his mug. "I'm worried about Ed. You think I should call her?"

"Yes! In fact, I'm surprised you've waited this long."

He put a hand up. "Okay, okay, I'll call her. Where's my phone?" He found it in his pocket and pulled it out. When he pressed a button, it didn't switch on.

"Something wrong?" asked Gina. She'd picked up her sudoku book again and looked ready to start a new page.

"Battery's gone. I have a charger in my office. Will you..."

She smiled. "I'll keep an eye on you. Don't worry."

Thanking her, he stood and left the conference room, shuddering as he crossed the floor outside. The office was dim, despite several lights being on, and it was getting increasingly cold. The heating was on a timer, and these were not business hours.

When will Mandy return?

Is she waiting for me to be alone again?

He glanced back to see Gina watching him through the glass window beside the conference room door. She should be able to see him enter his office, but to be sure, he left his door open.

His charger was plugged into a strip plug beneath his desk that was a pain to get at. He fitted the thin end to his phone and waited a minute for it to juice up, glancing constantly to make sure Gina could still see him. Once he got one per cent, he switched the phone on. It took thirty seconds, but eventually the operating system loaded and the screen started responding. He tapped his contacts and was about to scroll down to Ed, when the handset vibrated in his hand. A preview of a message slid down from the top of the screen.

He tapped the preview and opened the message.

Just had a massive barney with my landlord. Bastard turned up on my doorstep trying to change locks. I need to cool off, so I'm going to go to my parents in Bristol for a while. Not sure I'll be coming back. Tell Bernard I'll call him. Take care of yourself, Shane, and be careful. Ed x.

Shane put a hand to his forehead and groaned. After ten years of knowing each other, and hundreds of stories together, how could she just take off with only a text message? "You can't do this to me, Ed! We were working on this story together."

Well, there goes my one and only almost-friend. Guess I'm well and truly alone now.

That's what you get for trusting people.

Shane slumped in his chair and waited for his phone to charge a little more.

Shane called Ed three times in quick succession, but it went straight to voicemail each time. Frustrated, he left a message.

"Hey, Ed. I don't understand. How can you just be leaving? We were in the middle of something and you're running out on me? Just ring me, okay? Something happened to me at the office. It was... bad. If you hadn't slunk away you would've been here for it, so thanks for that. Call me when you get this. ASAP."

He stormed out of his office and rejoined Gina. "Think we need to call it a night. Ed isn't coming back, and I'm not sure where we go from here."

She nodded. "I agree. It's getting late."

When he checked his watch, it was exactly ten pm. "Yikes, is that the time? I should get you home. Where do you even live, by the way?"

"Right here in Redlake. I took the bus to get here."

"Really? Out of all the people you reached out to, the one who asked to meet just so happened to be in the same town as you?"

She grinned. "Almost like there're invisible forces guiding us, wouldn't you say?"

"Or coincidences happen every day."

"Is Ed okay?" she asked. "You stormed in here like you'd had a tiff."

"I couldn't get through to her. She sent me a message saying she's going to go stay with her parents. Seems like her landlord kicked her out or something. I can't believe how selfish she's being, running out on me like this."

Gina frowned at him. "She didn't seem a selfish soul to me. In fact, she seemed very kind."

"Usually, but she's left me in the lurch tonight."

"Maybe it's the other way around."

"What do you mean?"

"A woman in her thirties doesn't go to stay with her parents unless there's no other choice. If she's been kicked out of her home, then why aren't you helping her? Are you not friends?"

"We're colleagues."

Gina shrugged. "Then she owes you nothing. If you want my opinion, dear, I think it might be you who's selfish."

He scrunched his face up and tutted. "What? How am I selfish? I'm breaking my butt to save a bunch of random teenagers."

"And Ed followed you up and down the country today, trying to help."

"Yeah, well..." He sighed, grunted, and then shook his head. "Three bedrooms."

"Say again?"

"I have three bedrooms, and I didn't tell Ed she could crash at my place. She told me she was having issues with her landlord, but all I did was offer her my shitheap of a car. I'm a bad person."

Gina smiled at him. "But not so bad that you don't realise it. I'm sure you'll put things right."

"I will. I... I will."

His phone was still charging in his office, so he turned back to go get it. As he crossed the floor outside the conference room, he heard it ringing. He raced to answer it, hopeful it was Ed returning his call.

"Ed, I'm so sorry," he said, putting the phone to his ear.

"Shane!" It wasn't Ed.

"Sarah?"

"Shane, Evie's missing. I went to say goodnight, but she's not in her room. We had a fight and... and..."

He could hear she was crying. It made him clam up immediately. How the hell had he got so mixed up in his own head that he could be so unsympathetic to his own flesh and blood?

Because I resent her.

Is that true? Do I?

"Evie's probably just trying to upset you," he said. "Have you tried calling her friends?"

"Of course I have! Shane, she left a note on her door. It says she did something stupid and needed to get away. Shane, what the hell has she got herself into? Have you been putting nonsense in her head?"

Anger flared inside him. He almost lashed out but managed to stop himself. "No, Sarah, I haven't been putting nonsense in her head. I know I'm not an outstanding role model, but I only want what's best for Evie. Look, send me some details of her friends and I'll try to track her down, okay? It'll all be fine, I promise."

"Shane, she's really been going off the rails lately. I don't want her to ruin her life like... like..."

"I know," he said, cutting her off. "She won't. Send me the info and I'll find her."

"Maybe I should search her room. I didn't go inside. I just read the note on her door and panicked when I saw she was gone."

"No, don't overreact. Let me help. Send me the details of her three best friends. I guarantee one of them will know where she is."

There was a moment where his sister just sobbed down the line, but then she thanked him and ended the call.

Shane went back into the conference room, holding his phone as text messages started coming through from

Sarah like machine-gun fire, all with details of various friends.

Gina smiled at him. "Have you sorted it?"

"Not yet. Something else came up. I need to get you home so that—"

His phone rang again. This time, when he glanced at the screen, it was an unrecognised number. He answered the call. "Evie?"

"It's Millie. W-we spoke earlier. You bought me lunch."

"Oh, hey Millie. It's not really a good time right now, so I'm going to have to call you ba—"

"My grandma's here. She keeps following me around the house, and she has that strange look in her eyes again. I'm scared. Will you come? It's the proof you wanted."

"Where are your parents, Millie?"

"They went out to dinner and a show. I asked them not to, but they arranged it ages ago and told me I was being silly. You said I could call you."

Shane closed his eyes, feeling dragged in a dozen different directions. "Okay, Millie. Sit tight, okay? Try to stay away from your grandma until I get there."

"Okay. I... I'll lock myself in the bathroom. Will you come soon?"

"As soon as I can." He ended the call and stood there, not knowing what to do.

Gina stood up and touched his arm. "What is it?"

"That was the girl I met earlier. The one who's being visited by her grandmother. She's scared."

"Is her grandmother there now?"

"You heard me. I told her to keep away."

"We need to go help her."

He nodded. Of course they did, and yet... "I have to make another call first."

Evie's phone rang twice before she answered. "Uncle Shane?"

"Evie! Your mother's worried sick. Why did you run off?"

"I couldn't take being locked in my room on my own. I-I freaked out."

He shook his head, gripping the phone tightly in his fist. "Freaked out about what?"

"Nothing. It's nothing for you to worry about."

"Where are you?"

"With my boyfriend."

"You have a boyfriend? I never knew that."

She grunted down the phone. "I don't tell you everything. Anyway, I'll call mum and let her know I'm okay. Just chill out."

"No, Evie. Go home, or you'll be in big trouble. And what's with this note you left? What stupid thing did you do?"

"Nothing. I was just smoking weed and got paranoid. Bad trip, you know?"

"Evie? For fuck's sake."

"Hey, you're a drunk. Don't judge me."

Shane gasped, not knowing how to respond to that besides wanting to wring her neck. "I'm going to ignore your gross attitude, dear niece, because I love you. Go home and put your mother out of her misery. Right now. What you're doing isn't fair."

She huffed down the phone. "Fine. Whatever."

She ended the call.

Shane shook his head in disbelief. "What is happening tonight?"

"Family problems?" Gina asked, holding her tote bag.

"Niece problems."

He sent off a text to Sarah to let her know Evie was okay and coming home. At least he'd dealt with one crisis. Which one to deal with next?

His phone chirped with another text message. This one wasn't from Sarah; it was a reply from Ed. It simply read: *Screw you, Shane. The world doesn't revolve around you.*

Groaning, he immediately tried to call her, but it went straight to voicemail. He sent a text but had a sinking feeling she'd turned off her phone. "Damn it, Ed."

Gina looked at him. "Everything okay?"

He put his phone in his pocket and stood there. "Is there something in the air tonight, or are people just crazy?"

"People have always been crazy, Mr Mogg. Are you just catching up?"

"I reckon I might be. Come on, let's go. I have a feeling my night is just starting."

CHAPTER TEN

Millie was very much on Shane's mind, but her parents would surely be back soon. He would check in with her over the phone later to make sure she was okay. Ed, on the other hand, might be about to disappear forever. He had to convince her to stay. It was probably already too late.

I'm such a donkey.

He offered to drop Gina off at home, but she insisted on staying the course. Considering how much he kept getting things wrong today, having her along might be a wise choice. She could elbow him in the ribs every time he started making poor decisions.

He manoeuvred his Land Cruiser down a side street lined with takeaways and a bookies, then followed the road down to the end, where it turned into a car park surrounded by a row of modern redbrick flats. Nearly all of the windows were dark, the residents asleep. It boggled the mind to think a landlord might want to split one of the modest, two-bedroom units into multiple occupancy.

Whoever rented would get little more than a hamster's cage to live in.

Had Ed's cupidinous landlord actually changed the locks? When she'd said she was going to stay with her parents, had she meant tonight? Surely she wouldn't want to drive to Bristol in the late hours, not after the day she'd had?

It struck Shane that he'd never been here before. He only knew Ed's address because it had once been the site of a bowling alley that had closed its doors five years ago. The housing developers had crafted a statue out of old bowling balls and placed it at the entrance to the road, which had made the area a bit of a landmark for a while. Unfortunately, the statue lasted only two years before a refuse lorry backed into it.

He didn't know which flat was Ed's, but fortunately the doorbells were all labelled. Hurrying from one entrance to the next, he checked the names until he found one on the first floor of the middle building that read: *E. Hobbs*. He pressed the buzzer.

No answer.

He rang again.

Gina got out of the car and joined him in the recessed entryway. "No luck?"

"I don't know if she's gone to sleep or if she's ignoring me. I need to make sure she doesn't leave without me apologising first."

"Maybe it's best to let things be tonight."

He looked at Gina and nodded, but then turned and pressed the buzzer again. When there was still no answer, he tried Ed's neighbour, who answered immediately.

"Yes? Who is this?"

"Good evening, ma'am. My name is Shane Mogg. I'm trying to get hold of Ed. Can you let me in, please?"

"Who?"

"Ed? Edwina Hobbs?"

"Never heard of him."

"Her. She's your neighbour."

"Don't see much of 'em. Sorry, can't help you."

Shane bashed a fist against the brickwork. "Look, can you just buzz me in, please, so I can knock on her door?"

"No. I don't know who you are, and it's eleven o'clock at night."

"I'm aware of that. It's important."

"Sorry." The intercom hissed and went silent.

Shane clenched his fists and growled. "Bloody woman. What's her problem?"

Gina patted him on the back to calm him down. "We could be anyone, couldn't we?"

He grabbed the heavy metal-framed glass door and yanked on it. It rattled in its frame but was too strong to force open. Kicking only resulted in him hurting his foot.

"Mr Mogg! Calm down. You're going to do yourself an injury."

The intercom buzzed to life again.

"Ed?"

"No. It's me again. I can hear you down there, you know? My window's right above you. Get the hell out of here before I call the police."

"Just let me in!"

"You've got three seconds to leave, and then I'm calling."

"For what? I'm not doing anything."

"You're causing a disturbance."

"Only because you won't let me in, you greasy shrew."

"I'm calling them."

Gina pulled at his arm. "Come on. You tried but Ed's obviously not in. There's no need to pick a fight with a stranger."

Hissing, Shane stepped back from the door and glared up at the window above, wanting to see the woman who was being so obstinate. But the curtains were drawn, allowing only a slither of amber light to bleed through the gap in the middle.

"They're neighbours," he muttered to himself, thinking. "So that other window must be Ed's."

"What are you thinking?" Gina asked, sounding concerned.

Shane turned a circle, looking around. There was a grassy verge running between the pavement and the building's foundation. He quickly found several small stones embedded in the dirt and gathered them up.

"This isn't a good idea, Mr Mogg."

"Eh, I've had worse ones." He threw a stone and struck the centre of the windowpane that he judged to be Ed's. It made a resounding *clonk!* Pleased, he stood back on the pavement and waited for Ed to come to the window.

She didn't.

He threw two more stones, hitting the target with each one. *Clonk-clonk!*

Still no answer. At least, not from Ed.

"I'm calling them!" The annoying woman had opened

her window and was now leaning out. In or around her fifties, she had short-cropped blonde hair. "And I'm fetching John upstairs, so you better be gone by the time he gets his shoes on."

Shane pointed a finger up at her. "You're a real pain in my arse. Do you know that, lady?"

"Get out of here!" was her only reply as she slammed the window shut.

Gina pulled at Shane more insistently. "We really should get going. You can't help anyone if you spend the night in a cell."

"No one's getting arrested." He glared up at the window. He knew he was losing his temper, but it felt good when compared to losing his mind. His dead daughter had returned tonight, and this stupid woman wouldn't press a button for him.

"Even so," said Gina, "it's a distraction we don't need."

He huffed. "Fine. You're right, let's get out of here."

They turned around and got back in his car. Shane started the engine, just in case this John was real and actually came down looking for a fight, but he couldn't leave without trying to contact Ed one last time.

His phone was charging via a cable plugged into the cigarette lighter. He grabbed it and called Ed's number again.

The call went straight to voicemail.

All he could do was leave another message. This time, he tried not to just think about himself. It was a bizarre sensation.

"Ed? It's me. I don't know if you'll pick this up, but if

you do, I'm sorry. Whatever you need, I'm here. Also, Millie called. Her grandmother's back. I'm going to call her now, but if she can really offer us proof, then I'm going to make the trip tonight to go get it." He paused and took a breath. "Please call me, okay?"

He ended the call and turned to Gina, who was smiling at him. He'd already forgotten the words he'd just spoken, but they seemed to have got the old woman's approval at least.

Just call me back, Ed. Please.

Shane didn't know if he was making the right decision, but when he failed to get ahold of Millie, he decided he needed to go check on her. Her parents didn't exactly seem to be the attentive type, so who knew if they'd even come back from the show yet? They might even have gone to a club afterwards or stayed at a hotel.

Or they were already home, and Millie was safely asleep in her bed.

For his own peace of mind, he needed to make sure, and as close as he came to calling the police, he couldn't risk creating a circus in the middle of the night for possibly no reason. Millie's parents might not take kindly to be woken up by flashing lights.

Gina's coming along was a little awkward. A ninety-minute drive at midnight with an elderly ex-nun was a surreal turn of events, that was for sure, yet she had insisted on staying to help. "You shouldn't do this alone," she had said, before falling asleep in the passenger seat and snoring loudly. Probably for the best, seeing as how cold it was in the car.

It was nearly two o'clock when they arrived back on Millie's street. The same street where Hannah and Stefani had died mysteriously only two nights before. A part of him wanted to check on Miss Goodacre, to make sure she was all right, but a larger part of him decided it was best to leave the grieving woman alone. He had a habit of making things worse lately.

Lampposts illuminated the road, as well as several lights on the driveways of the various properties. Along with a smattering of bushy trees, it created a peaceful tableau of middle-class security. No one would ever think two of the properties were possibly haunted.

Shane parked up at the end of Millie's driveway and switched off the engine. Turning to Gina, he told her to stay in the car while he checked things out. She warned him to be careful, which put his hackles up because he hated being told what to do.

She's only concerned about me. That's not a bad thing.

A white Range Rover – a few years old – sat in the driveway, suggesting Millie's parents were home, which was a relief.

No police or ambulances. No cordons or flashing lights.

Millie must be in bed.

But she said she was going to tell her parents if her grandmother returned. If she did that, her parents would have shot out of the house like a rocket and gone to stay somewhere else. Somewhere without a ghost.

Something doesn't add up. Shane felt it in his tired bones.

He went back to the car and pulled his phone from the charger. He called Millie.

It rang.

And rang and rang.

No answer. No voicemail. Just a constant *ring-ring, ring-ring*.

"Come on, Millie. Answer and let me know you're okay." He stepped back onto the pavement and moved to the end of the driveway again. There was a danger of a neighbour seeing him and assuming he was up to no good, but at 2AM the residents were most likely all deep in slumber. It wasn't the kind of street where people partied past midnight. Not on a Monday night.

The phone continued ringing out. Shane grew tense, desperate to hear a voice on the other end. But Millie wasn't answering. Asleep, or...

What if she needs help? She said she was going to lock herself in the bathroom? Did she think her grandmother was going to hurt her?

She called me for help.

"Damn it! Answer my call, kid."

He paced up and down the driveway, nearly ready to wake everyone up just to make sure Millie was all right. It would take some explaining – a thirty-nine-year-old calling on a schoolgirl at 2AM – but what else could he do?

As he moved closer to the property, he realised he could hear Millie's phone ringing. Her bedroom must have been at the front of the house.

He looked up at the window above the garage.

But the ringing didn't seem to be coming from there. It

was close, but more at ground level. He tilted his head and homed in on the faint trilling. For a moment, he thought it was coming from inside the garage, but when he moved in that direction, it seemed to be coming from even further back.

The garden? Is Millie's phone outside?

There was side access next to the garage.

A wheelie bin sat in front of the gate, blocking it. It made a nice, flat platform on which to climb.

Am I really going to take things this far?

Her phone's ringing. I can hear it. Why isn't she answering?

"Damn it." He glanced back at Gina, who was peering out the passenger window at him, her eyes wide. She clearly didn't think he should be doing whatever he was thinking of doing, but before he could stop himself, he was leaping up onto the bin and fighting to keep his balance. It surprised him he could still pull off such a manoeuvre, but he couldn't ignore the shockwave of pain in his knees. He was getting old.

From up high, he was able to look right over the top of the gate.

The phone call rang off. It didn't go to answerphone, just went dead. To Shane's knowledge, you had to call the network to switch off your voicemail service. Why would Millie do that?

Maybe someone used to leave her not very nice messages. The kid's an oddball, and even in 2023, teenagers can still be nasty little shits.

Millie, you'd better be okay.

Shane was unwilling to risk climbing over the six-foot

gate, but luckily, he could reach over and grab the latch from his elevated position.

He unlocked the gate and hopped back down off the bin, sending another shockwave through his body, this time through the soles of his feet. He had to take a moment to hiss through the pain, trying not to make a racket as his pulse beat in his temples.

He pushed the gate open carefully.

Curiosity had evolved into trespassing.

The side access was a row of concrete slabs running alongside the edge of the house. An exterior door on the left led into the garage. Shane considered trying to get it open, but that would elevate his trespassing to breaking and entering, and that was a route he ideally didn't want to go down. Plus, he wasn't sure that Millie's phone was even inside the garage. To be sure, he rang her number again.

Ring-ring, ring-ring.

It was definitely coming from further ahead, past the garage and beyond the side access. The garden, just as he'd thought. It didn't make a lot of sense.

The only light came from a solar-powered LED light strip screwed into the wall six feet up on the side of the house. It wasn't bright enough to dispel the darkness, but it was enough to give shape to the various objects stacked up on the slabs. Some old roof tiles. A flat basketball. A clay plant pot big enough to hold a shrub or small tree. Shane crept past it all on his way to the garden.

The side access funnelled into a patio that wrapped around the rear of the property. There were two pairs of French doors at the back of the house, one on each side, with a large double window in the middle. Shane tiptoed and peered inside. He could make out the angular shapes of a large kitchen. No one was inside.

The ringing was coming from behind him.

He turned around.

Beyond the patio was a square-shaped lawn with a summer house in one corner. Next to the summer house was a large overhanging tree. Horticulture was no skill of his, so he didn't know exactly what species it was, but its thick branches started high and split off into numerous offshoots. The largest branch of all hung towards the ground at such an angle that it was practically vertical. An odd shape compared to the rest of the tree.

What is that?

No...

The silhouette wasn't a branch pointing towards the ground. It was a body, swaying gently back and forth. On the ground below, something flashed. A ringing phone.

"Please, no." Shane froze in place, trapped equidistantly between fight and flight.

He had to bite down on his tongue to push himself into action.

Placing one foot in front of the other, he moved across the lawn. The grass was soft underfoot, well tended and amply fed. Someone took pride in this garden. Millie's mother? Her father? Where the hell were they?

The body came slowly into view, a bleary grey blob becoming arms and legs, a head and torso. Then it became Millie.

Shane stopped in front of the girl and almost doubled over in pain, an invisible fist punching him in the guts. He fought against it and forced himself to look at her face. Her eyes were open – slightly bulging – and so was her mouth, the tip of her tongue peeking out. Other than that, she seemed peaceful. An object touched only by an invisible breeze.

She called me. She asked for my help.

I should've come right away.

"I'm so sorry."

It was only a matter of time before he puked up the pizza he'd eaten earlier, and his stomach contents on the ground at a crime scene wasn't desirable, so he had to go. He had to.

But it was difficult to pull himself away. Grief cemented him in place.

Not grief. Guilt.

It was easy to reconstruct events. Millie's parents must have returned home late, probably a little tipsy, and had gone straight up to bed, assuming their teenage daughter was already sound asleep. In the morning, they would notice her absence and begin to worry. Their search would eventually lead them to glance out into the garden.

They should've been around. Who leaves a teenager alone at night?

What the hell happened?

I know what happened. I knew and I didn't come right away.

"Such a pretty girl," said a voice right behind him, whispering directly in his ear.

He leapt in the air and spun around.

He was utterly horrified by what faced him.

A creature made of black and grey, with lidless eyes a maelstrom of madness and rage.

Grandma.

The old woman's broken teeth contorted into a grin as she stood there in the middle of the plush garden. A rancid odour, like wet faeces, wafted from beneath her mouldering nightdress.

Shane couldn't even blink. "Why... why did you do this?"

Millie's grandma reached out to him, a skeletal hand sticking out from festering flesh, finger bones piercing through the decaying tips. "I released her. I made the pain stop."

Shane staggered backwards to avoid death's grasp. He collided with Millie's cold, dead body swinging from the rope around her neck and yelped. The bough above her head creaked like a cellar door.

Grandma snatched at Shane again, hissing like a viper. Her sagging face elongated as if squeezed by a vice. Her skeletal body gave off fumes, a black veil surrounding her.

Shane tried to dodge away again, but his feet slipped on the soft grass. He hit the ground, trying not to wail, and his entire body quaked as he crawled desperately on his hands and knees.

"Come to me," said Grandma, her dark presence contracting and expanding. "Come to me and it all stops. Why..." She paused for a second as if struck by a jolt of confusion. "Why am I here?"

"I don't know," Shane whispered.

"It burns!" Grandma lunged across the lawn, flowing after Shane in a waft of putrid black smoke. There was no escape. No way to get up and run for safety. Even the moon seemed to desert him, removing all existence of light.

He rolled onto his back and put out his hands. "Please..."

Grandma loomed over him, her eyes like molten slag swirling with something unknowable. Her humanity had leaked away like blood from an artery, to be replaced by a soul of black ash. Was this death? Suffering and torment?

The dead thing opened its mouth, revealing a darkness beyond anything Shane had ever seen. Flies appeared out of nowhere, buzzing all around. "I will save you, child. I will make the burning stop."

Shane closed his eyes and wept.

A voice shouted over the top of him. "Get back!"

He opened his eyes and saw Gina. The old woman had appeared on the lawn and was now thrusting something out at Grandma, something that made the phantom shrink away like a snail retreating back into its shell.

A hissing shriek erupted from the centre of the black cloud. Noxious fumes billowed angrily into the night sky.

The moon returned.

Shane stared up at Gina as she stood over him like a sworn protector – albeit one who was trembling with terror. "M-M-Mr Mogg," she said. "I think we should leave."

He nodded, and to his surprise he was able to climb to his feet. Gina shoved him behind her, while continuing to hold the mysterious object out as a weapon. It glinted in the moonlight.

Her crucifix.

The one she had stolen fifty years ago from a Sicilian abbot.

Jesus saves.

Grandma kept back, hissing and spitting. The dark

aura around her contracted and expanded like a sickly black lung.

Shane and Gina backed out of the garden.

They re-entered the side access, and at the end of the slabs they passed through the gate and hurried down the driveway, rushing back towards the car. Shane leapt inside and started the engine, gibbering with relief when it immediately spluttered to life. His trusty old Land Cruiser.

Gina got in beside him. "Drive, Mr Mogg. It's coming after us!"

Grandma flowed out of the side gate like a squalling wind of volcanic ash, blotting out the light.

Shane pulled away from the kerb just as lights switched on inside Millie's house. Her parents were awake.

This is going to be the worst night of their lives.

Because I didn't help their daughter when she needed me.

Grandma howled, a black mesh fanning out to envelop the car.

Shane put his foot down, clutching the steering wheel so tightly that his knuckles cracked.

Grandma gave chase, a black hole of misery, but eventually she faded away as they exited the close and hit the main road.

I'm going to have a heart attack. Just like my dad.

I can't breathe.

"Are you okay, Mr Mogg? Are you hurt?" Gina was shaking like a leaf.

He shook his head, glaring through the windscreen at the road ahead, not daring to blink. "I am nowhere near okay. This madness has to stop."

"What do you suggest?"

"I suggest you and I find out exactly who Vita is. Then we're going to make the bastard pay."

Gina did the sign of the cross and clasped her glittery crucifix between her palms. "Amen."

CHAPTER ELEVEN

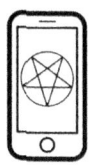

Neither of them spoke for a while, possibly ten or twenty minutes. Not that Shane didn't want to say anything. It was more that his mind was incapable of processing what in the fuckety fuck had just happened.

Millie was dead, strung up from a tree by her dead grandma – an apparently once decent woman who was now a vile, rancid abomination returned from the grave. If this was life after death, then it was worse than he'd ever imagined as either an atheist or a Christian. What of Heaven? What of everlasting peace?

"How did you know your crucifix would work," he asked, thirty miles from Millie's house. They were going seventy down a quiet M40, his halogen high beams slicing an orange cone in the road.

"I didn't. I just hoped."

"It was like something out of a movie."

"Whatever we're up against, it's unholy," she said. "We're going to need God on our side."

He shook his head and sighed. "This isn't real."

"Reality is ever-changing," said Gina. "Believe me, as an old woman I can attest to that. Never trust that tomorrow will play by the same rules as today."

Shane shook his head. "No, I won't accept it. I need proper answers. Everything has a reason, but... but not this. This is wrong. Another young girl is dead. Dead because she performed a stupid ritual online." He started to cry, his facial muscles spasming out of control. "She... she knew she was in danger, but I didn't believe her. Worse, when I *did* believe her, I didn't come straight away."

Gina looked at him. "We wasted less than an hour trying to find Ed. It wouldn't have made a difference. Don't blame yourself, Mr Mogg."

He beat a fist at the steering wheel. "I can't bear to think that she's suffering."

Gina took a moment, frowning. "You mean Mandy?"

He nodded. "I can't stop thinking about her. Emily too. Were they together in Heaven? Is Emily still up there now, in agony at having her daughter ripped away from her? Or have they been apart since the moment they died? Do we stay joined after death? Are we even ourselves any more? What are the fucking rules, Gina?"

She reached over and patted his hand as it gripped the steering wheel. "I know a place we can go, dear. A place I always go when I need answers. Take us back to Redlake, and I'll tell you where to go from there."

He looked at her, wanting to ask where on earth could provide answers to such mortifying, existential questions, but he found himself too tired to ask. Gina was a woman who had lived. Time to trust in her wisdom, because he sure as hell couldn't trust in his own.

So he headed back to Redlake, ready to get some answers.

An hour later, Gina gave him directions. Although he knew the town well, he had no idea where she was taking him until they arrived there. The Holy light and St Megrid's was a Catholic church near the Previs John Private Sixth Form College on Redlake's eastern boundary. It was the rich part of town, not somewhere Shane had ever spent much time.

The church was, like most Catholic structures, impressive. Built in the Gothic revival style, it had several sharp spires jutting out of a large square tower positioned at the back of the cruciform building. Outside the front entrance was a six-foot stone statue of Christ the Redeemer. As a once devout Anglican, Shane had never stepped foot inside a Catholic church, yet he could appreciate its beauty and history. Historical architecture had once been an interest of his, back when he had interests.

"Why did you bring us here?" he asked Gina as they sat in the car. "It's almost 4AM. No one's here."

"I have a key," she said.

He frowned at her. "Really?"

"I live nearby, so the pastor gave me a key to open up on occasions when his sciatica's causing him to run late. He won't mind us seeking a little guidance in the lonely hours."

"You come here a lot?"

"I'm an usher and a member of the choir." She said it proudly.

"And you're sure this is okay? I don't want to get in trouble with the Pope."

She rolled her eyes at him and opened the car door. "Come on, Mr Mogg. Let's go inside."

Not wanting to be alone, he got out and went after her.

True to her word, she produced a long brass key attached to a keychain from inside her tote bag. Her hand shook badly as she pushed it into the deep recess of the church's large wooden door, and Shane wondered if it was her nerves or something else.

Probably just age. I don't feel so steady myself.

They accessed the gloomy, deserted building via a high-roofed atrium with exposed timbers and then passed through a narrow narthex. Finally, they entered the nave – the main part of the church where people sat.

Shane took in the various holy paraphernalia. Close by, an ancient pedestal made of stone held an ornate font full of holy water. Hanging from the ceiling, further back, was something he thought was called a rood screen – a decorative wooden beam hanging above the altar and demarcating the beginning of a raised area known as the chancel. The various cherubic figurines adorning the ten-foot length of dark wood were probably worth a small fortune all by themselves.

Teak box-pews flanked the centre aisle, and a thin red carpet with floral designs covered the floor instead of tiles or wood. It lent the space a warm, casual atmosphere. Behind a white stone altar at the back was a rounded plaster recess with a painted statue of Michael, swan-like wings unfurled behind him. The archangel wore a sky-blue loincloth and nothing else. Bronze candelabras surrounded him in a semi-circle.

"It's beautiful," said Shane.

"A hundred and fifty years old," said Gina.

"The upkeep on this place must have cost a fortune. The Church never seems short of a penny, does it?"

"Don't be so cynical. The roof leaked in this place for six years before we found the money to mend it. You think the Church is immune to the sweeping hand of progress? The number of young people coming through the doors lessens every year. It brings me to tears some nights when I think about the future. A future without God."

"God's domain is the past," said Shane. "I don't see things improving."

"Even with what's happening? How can people deny Him now?"

"I have a feeling this will all be explained away somehow. Who's going to take ownership of a bunch of dead teens? The Church won't leap up and say it's proof of God, will they?"

Gina didn't answer. She strolled down the red carpet towards the altar. After a moment, he followed after her.

It was chilly inside the church, but not as cold as the Anglican chapels Shane remembered from his youth. Those old stone buildings had always been freezing in the cold months. Many had lacked modern heating, still burning oil and blasting hot air up through iron floor grates.

He hated to admit it, but it felt oddly comfortable being inside a church. Whatever he might presently believe – or not believe – the Church had always been a place of familiarity: of family, friends, and acceptance. Even if he didn't miss God, he often missed that sense of belonging, of being a part of a community. He had felt alone for so long now, even when surrounded by people.

I chose to be alone. I gave up on people.

No, I gave up on myself. Gave up on feeling.

Gina sat down in the front pew on the left. She folded her hands in her lap and closed her eyes. From the way her lips moved silently, she might've been whispering a prayer to herself. Shane remained quiet until she was done, and then she patted the bench beside her.

He sat down.

"It's been a while since I've been inside a church," he admitted.

"You stopped coming after what happened?"

"After I lost Emily and Mandy. I couldn't believe in God any more, or – I don't know – maybe I did still believe in Him, but I hated Him. That's how it started, I think. With hate. It eroded everything else."

Rather than comment, Gina sat quietly next to him. For a while, they both peered up at Michael's image behind the altar, the angel standing tall at the back of the chancel. Could not the archangel come to earth now and stop this evil from pervading? If Heaven existed, how could the dead return unrestrained?

Shane stifled a yawn and sat up straight. "I don't think Millie's grandmother was a bad person," he said. "So why did she end up the way she is? All twisted and violent?"

"I told you," said Gina. "The pain of being torn away from paradise is probably an agony we can't imagine."

"My daughter's suffering because I brought her back."

He flopped forward, head in his hands. "What have I done?"

Gina reached out and rubbed his back. "We'll find a way to put Mandy back to rest, Mr Mogg."

He rose back up and let his hands drop into his lap. "What if there is no Heaven or Hell, and we just drift around after we die, unseen and unfulfilled? Isn't it possible that all the ritual does is bring souls forward, back onto our wavelength? Doesn't that make more sense than there being an omnipotent, but indifferent, almighty power?"

"It's not for us to make sense of the universe. We're not supposed to understand the meaning of life."

"Mandy was two years old when she died, Gina. There's no meaning in that. It's just fucking chaos."

"I understand why you might think that." She turned to him and let out a sigh. The bags beneath her eyes were so dark they were obsidian. "I don't know what I can say to help you. Other than that I'm sorry."

He blew air into his cheeks and let it out in an exasperated rasp. His eyes were fuzzy with tiredness, and his body felt awash with pain and stiffness. Scratches and cuts covered his arms and face. He was a mess.

But somehow he laughed.

Gina frowned at him, a bemused smile creeping onto her lips. "What's funny?"

"Oh nothing. I'm just laughing at the irony of it all. I once believed in God so completely, followed all of His rules, but I lost my wife and daughter anyway. Meanwhile, my sister did everything she could to spit in His face and ended up with a daughter she never wanted."

"But I'm sure she loves Evie all the same."

Shane nodded. "It's a tough gig, but she does her best. By all rights, Sarah should be incapable of loving a child, but Evie means the world to her. Somehow, she learned how to be a mother without ever being taught."

"Your own mother was difficult?"

"She was a tyrant. I don't know if she was always that way, or if it was after my dad died, but she was a joyless woman who never hugged or kissed us or told us that she loved us. No, all she did was criticise and punish." He shook his head, feeling the spite rising up inside him. "Pleasing God was the only thing she cared about. It was an obsession. Actually, now that I'm older, I can see it for what it really was. Mental illness."

Gina grimaced. "Is that what you think religion is? Mental illness?"

"Everyone's a little mental, but I wouldn't blame it on religion. My mother probably would have obsessed over something else if not God. Anyway, I can't even truly complain, because it was Sarah who got the worst of it. Mother used to lock her in her room for weeks on end sometimes, only letting her out a few times a day to use the bathroom and eat some food. I used to hear her weep at night when I was trying to sleep. All the chances I had to say something or do something…" He let his head drop. "I was her big brother, but I used to stand by and let it happen, because… because I was just glad it wasn't happening to me."

"You were just a child, Mr Mogg, and parents have a hold over us. I've known six-foot beer-swilling brutes cowed by their overbearing mummies. You had no control over your upbringing. Only now can you effect the change you wish to see. Be a better brother today. Be a good uncle to your niece. Wounds heal, but only once you stop picking at them."

He ran his hands through his hair, fingers cold and scalp greasy. "I'm so tired, Gina. I just want to go to bed and wake up next week with this having all been a dream."

"Me too. I keep asking myself if I have dementia, but I think I'm disappointingly sane."

Shane leant back in the pew and rolled his neck back and forth while yawning. Once he was done, he stretched out his limbs and said, "We should go soon, Gina. I can barely think any more. How about we rest here for ten more minutes and then go get some sleep? I'm terrified to be alone, but I'm going to end up in a coma eventually if I don't lie down. Maybe after we've rested we can attack this thing from a fresh angle."

She nodded. "Sounds like a plan, but make the most of this time, won't you? You came here looking for answers. This place can provide them."

"I'm all ears."

They sat in silence for a little longer. Gina closed her eyes and muttered another prayer, but even with recent events, Shane couldn't bring himself to beseech God. He'd witnessed evidence of evil, not of good. If anything, he had reason only to believe that the Devil was real.

He glanced over at Michael's statue and decided that while he wouldn't call on God, he could tolerate calling on an underling.

So what good are you, huh? Where are you and the other angels? Why not come to earth and solve famine and war and disease? Instead, you put it all on us. Free will, huh? A gift to humanity? More like God left his children unsupervised and surrounded by sharp objects.

Michael stared back at him through painted blue eyes.

A shadow moved across the bottom of the statue. Shane leant forward in the pew and squinted. He made out a slender shape. It seemed to move ever so slightly, slinking past Michael's sandalled feet.

The shadow had a sheen to it.

Like hair.

Someone was kneeling at the base of the statue, worshipping the archangel.

Shane shifted to the very edge of his seat, straining his eyes further to make out more detail.

The stranger was a child.

A child with dark hair.

Mandy.

Shane's dead daughter twisted her neck all the way around to look at him, while her body remained facing forward, kneeling at the archangel's feet. There was a glint in her eye, and she smiled with a mouthful of tiny, jagged teeth.

"Gina?" said a voice. "What are you doing here?"

Gina leapt up beside Shane, stiff and alert. "F-Father? It's the middle of the night."

A thin, elderly man appeared from an antechamber at the side of the chancel and moved in front of the elevated stone altar atop it. Dressed in jeans and a thick blue jumper with black leather elbow pads, his hair was so grey it was almost white. Gina had called him Father. Was he a priest here?

Where did Mandy go? I saw her.

Didn't I?

I'm so tired.

Shane peered at the base of the statue for his daughter, but she was gone. Michael continued to stand watch silently, a witness to nothing.

"I'm aware it's the middle of the night, Gina," said the elderly man. "That's why I asked *you* what you're doing here."

"Oh, yes, sorry, Father Michaels. I brought my friend here because he's in need of solace. He's... been dealing with a death."

Father Michaels looked down at Shane from the chancel, examining him suspiciously. "You look like you've been dragged through a hedge backwards, my friend."

Shane got up and patted himself down before standing to attention. He glanced back and forth, searching for his daughter, but he still couldn't see her. Was it because he wasn't alone like in the bathroom at *Splatt!*? "I... I was in a car accident. I'm sorry, Father. Gina assured me it was okay to be here. For where two or three gather in my name, there am I with them."

Father Michaels nodded slowly. "Matthew, I believe?"

"Chapter eighteen, verse twenty."

"Impressive. Well, it's not exactly routine for parishioners to turn up in the dead of night and let themselves in, but I can see you were simply praying. I suppose I'll start my duties a little early today."

Gina cleared her throat. "Um, Father Michaels, how did you know we were here?"

He raised an eyebrow at Gina and chuckled. "Oh, yes, you wouldn't know, would you? I had one of those what-do-you-call-its installed last week. An Everstech security camera. It sent an alert to my phone when you approached the entrance. When you reach my age, it doesn't take much to wake you."

"I apologise for waking you, Father."

"There are worse sins, Gina. You're forgiven. If you or your friend have need of me, I'll be in the vestry."

"Thank you, Father."

Shane nodded. "Yes, thank you, F…"

Something moved in the chancel, a shadow flitting by behind the altar. Father Michaels was unaware of it, but he obviously noticed the sudden apprehension on Shane's face. "Is everything okay?"

Shane threw out an arm. "Get away!"

"What on earth are you—"

Mandy leapt at Father Michaels from behind and took him entirely by surprise. He stumbled off the chancel and crashed onto his hands and knees below. Somewhat absurdly, he glared up at Gina as he gasped in pain, as if he assumed he was a victim of some kind of ambush.

Gina cried out in horror.

Shane froze.

Father Michaels screamed.

Mandy bit into the side of the priest's neck, tearing apart veins and sinew with her baby teeth. Her little hands wrapped around his shoulders and clamped his arms by his sides so that he couldn't struggle or get up, infinitely stronger than a toddler should be.

Shane yelled out. "Mandy! Stop!"

A sick, gurgling sound heralded a torrent of blood spewing from Father Michael's mouth as he fought desperately to yank the dead toddler from his back.

But he was fading fast.

Shane broke free from his inaction and raced to help the priest, but when he got close, Mandy hissed and swiped a sharp-clawed hand at him. All the while, she clung on to the priest with the other hand and both feet. She was wearing a dirty yellow onesie that Shane realised was the one she'd been wearing in the back seat of the car when she drowned. It was muddy around the collar and stained with blood. Her hair was lank and tangled with leaves from the river.

She's frozen in time, the moment of her death.

What must she have thought, strapped in her car seat as the ice-cold water flooded over her? Did she call out for her mummy?

Did she call out for me?

Shane screamed in anguish, his chest and lungs heaving. He threw himself at Father Michaels and grabbed Mandy, his arms enveloping her tiny body and yanking her away. She squirmed and thrashed, small but impossibly powerful. Within seconds, she had broken from his grip and heaved herself to the floor, landing like a cat on her hands and feet.

Father Michaels sprawled in the middle of the aisle, blood gushing from his neck, his arms stretched above his head as if he were trying to breaststroke his way forward. Then he went still.

"God save us," said Gina, stumbling against a box pew and almost knocking herself over.

Shane fixated on his daughter, watching her scramble about like some kind of wild animal. She crouched on all fours, glaring at him through eyes full of black fire. Like Grandma, her body gave off dark fumes.

"M-Mandy? Sweetheart? It's me, Dada." He put his hands out and crouched to her level. "No one wants to hurt you."

"Get back," said Gina. "Mr Mogg..."

"It's okay," he said. "I just want to talk to her."

"She's not listening."

Shane ignored Gina and focused on his daughter. "Mandy-Marble, do you remember me?"

For a second, the darkness receded from her eyes. Her body relaxed, although she remained crouched on all fours. "Dah-da."

"Yes! Yes, sweetheart, it's me! It's your dada."

"Hurts..." The darkness returned.

Mandy raced towards him, lolloping on hands and feet – more ape than human.

Shane faced a choice. Did he fight his own daughter? Punch and kick her and try to hold her down?

Could he do that?

No.

He dodged into the aisle, avoiding Mandy just as she attempted to pounce on him. His foot struck Father Michaels, and he almost tripped over the priest's body, but he let momentum carry him forward into a run.

Mandy screeched, redirected herself, and gave chase.

I can't fight her. I can't hurt her.

I can only run.

Gina yelled out. "Mr Mogg!"

But Shane kept on running, terrified and heartbroken and tired to the point of collapse. There was nowhere to go except straight down the centre of the nave. At the end of the aisle, he could rush through the narthex and head outside. Perhaps that would be enough to send Mandy away. Or at least give him more room to escape.

He made it past the final pews.

Mandy leapt onto his back.

He staggered forward, trying to stay on his feet. But it was impossible. The sudden weight on his shoulders caused him to overbalance, and he fell headfirst into the stone pedestal holding the church's font. He struck it so hard that it cracked in the middle and the heavy upper part gave way.

Shit!

Shane came down hard on his front with Mandy on his back. He instinctively curled up, anticipating having his skull crushed by solid stone.

The font tilted precariously to the right beside, and the heavy circular basin toppled over. Shane closed his eyes, waiting for his head to split in two, but the basin hit the ground beside him and broke into two half-moons. The impact sent cold water sloshing everywhere.

Mandy hissed. Her weight disappeared from Shane's back and he was able to roll over, winded and disorientated.

His dead daughter recoiled, clawing at her face and hair. The black smoke coming off her parted into narrow ribbons, fading in and out of existence. She was soaked with water from the broken font.

Holy water?

Are you serious?

Shane's dead daughter continued to claw frantically at herself. She started to dissipate, evaporating into black vapour. The last part of her to disappear was her face. She glared at Shane with such hatred that it horrified him that such a force could exist. It was beyond human emotion. It was primal. A spiritual need to destroy and defile.

That thing isn't my daughter.

Shane collapsed onto his back, panting. He closed his eyes and immediately felt sleep drag at him. It would be so easy to just give up and allow unconsciousness to take him. Let them drag him out of there on a trolley and dump him in the loony bin. Three meals a day, twenty-four-hour security? It had to be better than the madness of the real world.

It was several minutes before Gina approached him. He still had his eyes closed, so he didn't know she was standing over him until she spoke.

"Shane?"

"I'm okay. Are you?"

She stood unsteadily, hand over her chest and visibly shaking. "I'm not sure what to do. Father Michaels…"

"There'll be footage of us on his Everstech account. We're going to get the blame for this."

"Should we call the police? Try to explain?"

Shane sat up and rubbed at his eyes. He had more scratches from being attacked, once again, by his dead daughter, but nothing that needed urgent care.

My daughter who was just banished – exorcised – by holy water.

Where is she now? Where has she gone?

"I'll call the police," said Shane, "but only once we get out of here. We can't find Vita and stop him if we're arrested."

"We can tell them what happened."

He rolled onto his knees and crawled over to a pew to pull himself up. "What? Tell them a dead two-year-old chewed a hole in Father Michael's neck?"

"We... we can say it was an animal. A rabid dog."

Shane nodded, as unsteady on his feet as she was. "We can think about it, but for now we need to get out of here. It'll be a while before the police gain access to Father Michael's phone and his accounts – days even – so we have some time left to stop what's happening. We can't let kids keep on performing Nomon's Ritual. Hundreds could die. Thousands. It's up to us, Gina. Us!"

Gina was panting, but after a moment, she nodded slowly. "You're right. For whatever reason, God has called upon you and me to fix this. No one else sees what's happening. No one else understands."

"This isn't God," said Shane. "It's me and you and no one else. If God wants to lend a helping hand at some point, then by all means, but until then, we're on our own."

He turned around and exited the church, leaving behind yet another dead body.

CHAPTER TWELVE

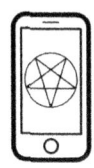

Shane collapsed outside the church, his legs unable to support his weight any longer. The next body part to mutiny was his stomach, spilling its frothy contents all over the pavement. Gina stood beside him but didn't help. She was too old to get down on the floor, so she just waited for him to recover. He retched several times more before he could get up, but even then, he was unsteady on his feet.

Gina had to help him to the car.

He saw his reflection in the passenger window and groaned. His hair was soaked from the holy water, dark and flat against his head. Thick bags underscored his eyes while scratches crisscrossed his stubbly cheeks. The weight of several deaths weighed upon him, the most recent worst of all.

I watched a man die. A priest.

It happened so fast. A life snuffed out in seconds.

Because I brought my daughter back from the dead. Mandy has blood on her innocent soul now.

"Fuck!" Shane didn't know it was coming, but suddenly he was a fire hydrant spewing rage. It came right up from his feet, through his entire body, and out of his mouth. Every cell in his body bellowed hysterically, trying to tear itself free of his flesh and assault the very fabric of existence. "Fuck, fuck, fuck!"

Gina reached out to him, but he shrugged her away. "Mr Mogg? Be quiet!"

"Why is life like this? Why does it have to hurt? I did everything right. Everything! I allowed love into my heart, tried to be a good man, and it tore me apart. It fucking ruined me!" He looked up at the sky, the pitch-black of night taking on the subtlest tones of blue – a threat of approaching dawn. "Fuck you, God! Fuck you. Why did you take them from me?"

"Mr Mogg, please calm down."

But he couldn't. All the pain inside him, trapped and festering for a decade, was finally oozing out like pus from a boil. He needed to get it all out or the rot would return.

But if he stood there screaming, eventually someone would come. Probably the police. He had to calm down.

He caught a breath and held it. Gina stood anxiously before him, a sweet old woman who just wanted to help. "I-I miss them," he spluttered. "I miss them so much."

"Oh, Mr Mogg, come here." She reached out and grabbed him firmly, probably using all of her strength just to keep him from resisting. "I know you miss them, dear. I know you do."

And just like that, Shane was a child in a mother's arms. Except Gina wasn't his mother, and his real one had never held him like this. He sobbed and wailed, not caring about who in the world might hear. His soul vibrated inside his chest, shedding its agony and loss, only to re-inhale it and shed it all over again. It was impossible to be free of it, but every sob brought him a heartbeat of peace.

His agony became a dull pain. His sobs turned to heavy breathing. Gina's frail arms continued to envelop him, providing a warmth he'd never felt before. A warmth he felt on the inside.

"Come on," she said soothingly. "Let's get you inside the car. It's all out now. Everything's going to be all right."

He didn't believe that for one minute, and yet he did feel better. Lighter.

Pulling the key from his pocket, he unlocked the Land Cruiser and got in behind the steering wheel. He put his hands on his lap for a moment and tipped his head back, taking in several deep breaths. Every second brought him a little extra strength – revitalised him a tiny bit more. He had gone an entire night without sleep, but his ordeal wasn't over yet. There was still work to do. Young lives depended on it.

"I need to call Ed," he said.

Gina nodded. "You need your friend. I understand. Call her."

And so he did.

But Ed still didn't answer. Once again, he left a voicemail, only this time he told her how much she meant to him, and that he would be devastated if she left. He ended the call by saying she was his friend and that he loved her.

"How did that feel?" Gina asked, patting him on the knee and smiling sympathetically.

"I feel vulnerable and stupid and – strangely – a little

angry at myself, but... it also feels good. Like a relief?"

"Bearing one's soul is never easy. I'm proud of you, dear."

That brought more tears. "Shitting hell. What's happening to me?"

"The past is catching up with you. Come on, we need to leave here before the world wakes up."

"You're right. What time is it?" He looked at his watch, which had cracked at some point during the night. "Jeez, 5AM. Do you need me to take you home?"

"I go wherever you go, Mr Mogg. We're a team."

"Then perhaps it's time you stopped calling me by my surname."

"Okay, Shane. What's our next move?"

"I... I want to call my sister. Is that okay?"

Gina looked out of the window towards the church, where a dead priest lay inside. "Well, I hate to stand in the way of an emotional breakthrough, but can you make it quick?"

"Of course. I... I'm just worried that I'm only going to get one chance at this. The future doesn't exactly fill me with hope, so I need to get this off my chest before any more shit hits the fan. Also, I haven't been this sober in a while."

Gina nodded at the phone in his hand. "Call her. Wake her up and tell her you love her."

Shane made the call. To his surprise, despite the unsociable hour, Sarah answered immediately. "Shane? Is that you?"

"Yeah. Sarah, I need to tell you some– "

"Evie didn't come home last night."

"What? She didn't come home? Why didn't you call me?"

"I didn't want to worry you, and..."

He frowned against the phone. "And what?"

"I didn't want you making things worse."

"What? How would I make it worse, Sarah?"

"By making me feel like a bad mother." She sounded tired. "By judging me and just generally being a prick. I can't deal with that right now."

Shane opened his mouth to speak, but no words came out. It took several seconds to regain his voice. "H-have you heard from her at all?"

"No. Shane, I searched her room. There's blood. I... I don't know where it's come from."

The world was spinning. It was one thing after another, making everything too difficult to bear. He felt like he was trying to swim his way through quicksand. "I'm on my way."

Shane made it to his sister's house in under fifteen minutes. Dawn was fast approaching, but the world was still asleep.

Except for Sarah. Sarah was waiting on the doorstep as if she were afraid to go inside her own home. In a dressing gown and slippers, she looked fifty instead of thirty-five.

He pulled up on the edge of the driveway and switched off the car. For a moment he just sat there, not wanting to get out. Why would there be blood in Evie's room? So many beautiful young girls had died in the last seventy-two hours; he wouldn't be able to bear it if something had happened to Evie.

"Can you do this?" Gina asked him. "You've been through a lot, on zero sleep."

"I have no choice. If Evie's in trouble, I'm as responsible as anyone else. She looks up to me, and I haven't taken that seriously enough."

Gina pulled her bag sluggishly out of the footwell. She looked in desperate need of sleep. "You want me to stay in the car?"

"No, please come with me."

She smiled and got out of the car with him. Sarah was understandably confused when she saw her brother heading towards her with a woman almost twice his age.

"This is my friend, Gina," he explained. "She's been helping me with a story. It's too complicated to explain."

"Hello, dear. I'm sorry to intrude."

"It's... it's okay, I guess." Sarah's voice was hoarse. She'd obviously been crying, and she was visibly tired.

Shane went and surprised her with a hug. "I'm sorry you didn't feel you could call me."

"I should have. Maybe you would've found her by now."

"We don't know anything bad has happened, so let's try to stay positive. Let me see her room, Sarah. There might be another note or something."

"You can look, but there's nothing except..." She shook her head.

"The blood? Show me."

Like a zombie, Sarah led him into the house and upstairs. Gina stayed in the hallway, teetering wearily. Shane wondered where the old lady got her strength.

The journey across the short grey-carpeted landing was like walking to a funeral. Neither he nor his sister spoke.

How much blood? What did Evie do to herself?

Or did someone hurt her?

Sarah opened Evie's bedroom door and then turned away as if she couldn't bear to look inside. Shane had to steel himself to enter, his stomach in knots.

It wasn't as bad as his imagination had made out, but it was still serious enough for him to be concerned. The duvet on Evie's double bed had been pulled back, revealing several substantial dark red stains on the bedsheet. There were also several droplets on her soft pink carpet. Finally, Shane spotted a bloody fingerprint on the clean white desk underneath the window. Evie had been bleeding profusely enough to leave multiple stains.

"It was the drops on the floor I noticed first," said Sarah, stepping into the room behind him. "Then I pulled back the covers. It's bad, right?"

He rubbed at the stubble on his chin while he thought about it. "I don't think it's so bad that we need to fear the worst. It's a lot of blood, but it might have come from a nosebleed for all we know."

Sarah put a hand against her face and shook her head. "I should've called the police right away. She's cutting herself."

The mention of the police sent a shudder up his spine, but he knew the situation was fast approaching the need to call upon them. "Why do you think she did something to herself?"

Sarah hugged herself, obviously trying to fight back tears. "Look in her drawer. In her desk."

He frowned, wondering what she wanted him to see. At first, when he checked inside the drawer, he saw only ordinary things – a stapler, some scraps of paper – but then he spotted what she must have wanted him to find.

He picked up the small metal scissors and inspected them. Dark red stains along the blades weren't from rust.

"She's been cutting herself," said Shane, echoing his sister's words as he closed his eyes and tried to stay calm. "Damn it, Evie."

"Kids do that when they're in pain, right? My little girl is suffering, and I didn't even know it. I failed her. That's what you're thinking, right?"

He placed the scissors down on the desk and marched over to his sister. Looking her in the eye, he grabbed her by the shoulders. "This entire world is a fucking circus, sis. You could be the best mother in the world and Evie would still be vulnerable to the pressures society piles on young girls. She's lucky to have you. Any kid would be."

That seemed to be like a knife in her ribs. She doubled over and sobbed. He rubbed at her back, which only made her shudder.

"I'm sorry," he said. "I should've been here more for you. Instead, I've made life harder. It's because you remind me of so many painful things. Things I've been trying to blot out. Things that were never your fault. Our mother was a fucking lunatic, Sarah. It's a miracle you ended up giving Evie a normal, loving home. You should be proud of yourself."

She straightened up, tears streaming down her face. "Are you messing with me? Why are you saying all this, Shane? You don't give a shit about me."

Right then, he saw the anguish on his sister's face, how abandoned she must have felt all these years. He saw how she feared him as much as she loved him – the same kind of relationship they had both had with their mother. "I'm saying it because I mean it, Sarah, and because I should. You needed me as a kid, and you need me now. It's time I started being a big brother. So we're going to find Evie, okay?"

She nodded, sniffed back snot. "Thank you."

"Don't thank me, I'm a prick. Okay, let's think about this. You called all of Evie's friends, I'm assuming?"

"Everyone I know of."

"What about her boyfriend?"

She flinched. "What boyfriend?"

"You didn't know either, huh? When I called her earlier – last night – she said she was with her boyfriend. He must've talked her into staying instead of coming home." He snarled and clenched his fists. "Little shit. When I find him, we'll be having words. And God help him if he's a lot older."

Sarah put a hand to her face. "She's repeating all of my mistakes, Shane. You must be loving this."

He shook his head, frustrated. It was too much to immediately expect her trust, but it still hurt that she thought so little of him. "Nothing about this makes me happy, Sarah. Listen, Evie's a smart kid – and you two aren't the same. She has no reason to rebel like you did."

"I'm tough on her. Maybe too tough."

"You're not. Look, does she keep a diary or anything?"

She pulled a face. "Kids don't actually keep diaries, Shane. I know you did, but you were weird."

"I was creative. And I became a journalist, so it kinda worked out for me."

"Writing stories about drop bears and cursed Tamagotchis? When do you get your Pulitzer?"

"Hey! We're not doing that any more, okay? New leaf."

"Sorry. Force of habit."

He chuckled. If things got much worse, he might not get many more chances to laugh, so he gave himself a moment to enjoy it. Murdered priests, dead girls... he had a feeling there would be very little room for levity ahead.

Sarah pointed at Evie's desk. "She has a laptop. I don't know the password though."

Shane turned and studied the small charcoal-coloured laptop sitting on the clean white desk. "Let me take a look."

He opened up the computer and the screen came to life after a few seconds. It was the familiar Windows login screen, asking for a password.

"I've tried everything I can think of," said Sarah.

Shane pulled out the wheeled chair underneath the desk and sat down in front of the laptop. Now was his chance to find out how well he knew his niece. He had thought Evie trusted him with everything, but how wrong he had been. Secret boyfriends and cutting herself...

Little shit.

He tried a couple of obvious password guesses, like Evie's name followed by her date of birth, as well as the obligatory "password", but they didn't work. It would take a little more elbow grease than that.

What would she put as a password?

She's a lazy teen, and not one particularly concerned about data security.

Favourite band? Favourite TV show?

"When did she get the laptop, Sarah?"

"About a year ago. It's new."

He nodded. That was good. It meant Evie might've set the password recently, which meant he only had to guess one of her current interests.

His fingers hovered over the keyboard.

He began to type.

H-a-r-r-y S-t-y-l-e-s.

Incorrect Password.

"Damn it." *No wait. I doubt she cares about grammar enough to use capitals—*

h-a-r-r-y s-t-y-l-e-s.

Incorrect Password.

—or a space.

h-a-r-r-y-s-t-y-l-e-s.

There was no fanfare. No congratulatory jingle or fancy graphics. The desktop just appeared with a smattering of icons and a background of what looked like a foppish boy band.

Sarah gasped. "You got in? What was her password?"

"You want me to tell you?"

"Actually, no. I'd be tempted to use it. We're already invading her privacy, but at least we have a good excuse right now."

He wasn't sure he would show that kind of restraint. As a journalist, he had a deep-seated desire to snoop. "Okay," he said, cracking his fingers out over the keyboard. "First thing I always do when I log on is check my emails. Let's take a look."

There was a little blue and white envelope at the

bottom of the screen, some third-party app that Shane was unfamiliar with. When he clicked it, it opened up just like any other client, showing a sidebar of email subjects and dates alongside a larger window displaying a preview of whichever message was selected. He went through them one by one, starting with the newest.

A couple of emails from shopping websites, a penis-enhancement scam that really was targeting the wrong victim, and a few messages from an educational platform that her school must have used to pass on homework and memos.

There was nothing helpful.

He checked the trash and found nothing there either.

Sarah stood over his shoulder. "Have you found anything?"

"Nothing yet, but don't panic. I'm not finished yet. I'm sure we can find some clue as to where she is."

His next trick was beautiful in its simplicity.

He opened up Eversearch and was presented with a query box. Into it, he simply typed 'A'.

Again, not being concerned with privacy, Evie had no problem with the browser providing autosuggestions – as well as historical searches.

Aardvark sexual reproduction diagram.

Alice, Darling imdb.

All the small things.

Amy Winehouse not dead.

Am I fat?

Am I pregnant after missing two periods?

"Oh!" Shane grimaced. "Oh, shit."

CHAPTER THIRTEEN

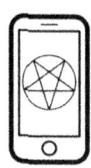

He considered clicking away but changed his mind. For years he'd believed he and Evie were a team – but that had been wrong. It was he and his sister who were supposed to be on the same page. Sarah needed to know what her daughter was up to.

She swore out loud when she saw the search suggestion, something she rarely did, even in her rebellious days. "Shane, she can't be pregnant. She can't ruin her life like I did." She covered her mouth and turned away, ashamed by what she'd just said out loud.

Shane jumped up and grabbed her, pulling her into a hug. "Hey, it's okay. I get it. Life is complicated."

"I love her so much, Shane, but sometimes she feels like my biggest screw-up. If only I'd waited… I-I could've been a much better mother."

"Don't you think a million mums have had the same thought? Life doesn't always go to plan, Sarah, but that doesn't make it any less worthwhile."

"I'm going to kill him, Shane. Whoever this lad is that's leading her astray."

He nodded. "Damn straight. He's taken my job."

"Ha! You drive me crazy, Shane, but it means a lot that you're so close to Evie, especially after…"

He swallowed, awash with emotion. "It's okay. You can say it."

She hugged him tightly, in a way she hadn't since they were kids. "I'm so sorry for Mandy and Emily. I saw it break you, but I didn't know what to do to help you. Every time I tried to get close, you pushed me away."

"I was angry. Angry you got to keep Evie, when you hadn't even planned for her. Truthfully, I've been resenting you ever since you left home and got away from Mother. You abandoned me."

"I… I'm so sorry."

"No, you did nothing wrong. I could have left too – there was nothing stopping me – but I'm just not as strong as you. I let Mother dominate my entire existence – and for what?"

Sarah shook her head. "She was messed up. I don't think she could help it."

"You know what makes me angriest of all? It's that even after I followed all of her rules, I lost everything anyway. None of it mattered. I never pleased God. I never got His blessing."

Sarah took a deep, hitching breath. She was as exhausted as he was, probably even more so, but she managed to lift her head and smile at him. "You were a good dad, Shane."

He felt like falling to the floor. It was difficult to get

everything out in the open when all he wanted to do was pass out in a comfy bed.

But it is out in the open now. We can finally move forward.

Sarah can visit me in prison after I'm nicknamed 'the priest killer'.

She shook her head at him. "Shane? What are we going to do about Evie? If she's pregnant?"

"There are worse things than having a kid. We just need to make sure she's happy and healthy and supported. Whatever else happens is just life being life. At least you still have her, Sarah. Don't take that for granted, trust me."

"I won't." She rubbed her face, her cheeks pale and her eyes red. "Shane, what happened to you tonight? It looks like you got into a fight with a bear. Don't get me wrong, it seems to have beaten a new personality into you, which is great, but... are you okay?"

It was more like an undead two-year-old than a bear.

"It's been a rough night. The worst of my life, in fact, besides the day I lost Mandy and Em. Yesterday morning, I started researching a story about kids on Clip Switch, so that I could write an article for a magazine on life support. It didn't pan out as expected."

"You mentioned Clip Switch earlier? What's going on?"

"Something bad. In fact, I need to check something."

He went back over to Evie's laptop and typed in the address for Clip Switch. The black and orange homepage came up immediately – already logged in.

"Thank you, sign-in cookies." He looked over his shoulder at her. "You know, it's ridiculously easy to invade an entire person's life these days. Get into someone's phone and you can catch a glimpse of their bank accounts, their fetishes, contact details for every human being in their life, their hobbies, their health, their calendar, their schedule. It's frightening. Steal a person's bank card and you can tap away a hundred quid in two seconds without leaving a trace. Technology is going to be the death of us."

"You're still an optimist, I see. What happened to letting life happen?"

"Life is the absence of technology. Life used to be kids hanging out at the park and riding their bikes. Now they do stupid dances in front of a camera so other kids will be jealous of a bunch of numbers ticking up on a screen. Hell, I was perfectly okay with video games – at least they tax the brain and imagination a little. Today's youth though... jeez."

"You sound like an old man."

"I feel like one." He moved over to the 'VIDEOS' tab and clicked on it. His heart froze in his chest while he waited for the page to load.

Two dozen thumbnails loaded in a grid. About half of them featured Evie in front of a camera. He checked the labels, dreading what he would find.

Water bucket challenge.
Birdy talk.
Amber Heard lip-sync dog bee challenge.
Killer klown murder lip-sync.
South Park Cartman stitch.
Worldwide privacy tour.
Zombie Dance.

It went on and on, nonsensical names for nonsensical

videos. He opened a few to double-check, but none showed Evie performing Nomon's Ritual. It was just her dancing, lip-syncing, or pulling weird facial expressions in reaction to some other video playing on the screen. He didn't see the appeal to any of it.

"What are you looking for?" asked Sarah, standing behind him with a hand on his shoulder. He already felt the emotional barriers between them slipping away.

"It doesn't matter. Everything's fine. These are all just normal videos; nothing to be alarmed about."

She leant over his shoulder and stared at the screen. "Wait... this isn't her account."

"What? Sure it is? She's in half these videos."

"Yes, but that screen name... it's different to the one I set up for her."

"You set an account up for her?"

"I had to. You have to be over eighteen to make money from ads... or something like that. I had to use my credit card to verify. Anyway, Evie has another account. This must be the one she used before I set up the new one."

Shane studied the thumbnails again, this time checking the date stamps. There hadn't been a new upload in over three months.

With a groan, he hovered the cursor over the top right of the screen where it said ACCOUNT MANAGEMENT. As soon as he took his finger off the trackpad, a drop-down menu opened. It displayed two usernames. The top one was highlighted in blue: TopzMogg27.

The one underneath was greyed out: TheEvieReel.

"That's the one," said Sarah. "TheEvieReel."

Shane's hand was shaking as he lowered his fingertip

back to the trackpad. He clicked on the greyed-out username and it turned blue. Video thumbnails for the new account started to populate. Hundreds of them.

The most recent video had been posted two nights ago. One night after Stef and Han had died on camera. He clicked the thumbnail and loaded the video.

Then watched in horror as Evie stood in front of the camera and spoke Latin.

The words to Nomon's Ritual.

"No…" Shane shook his head. "No, no, no."

"What is it?" Sarah sounded panicked. "Shane, what's wrong?"

He looked up at his sister and tried to find the words. How did he tell her that her daughter had summoned the dead, and that whatever came back was going to try to kill her? "I'm going to tell you something crazy," he told her. "And you have to believe me."

After calling Evie a dozen times and not getting an answer, Shane told Sarah about everything that had happened since 9AM yesterday morning when he'd picked up Evie late for school. He did so in the kitchen, so that Gina could sit with them and confirm everything he was saying. Of course, Sarah was incredulous, but as he showed her various news reports about Stefani and Hannah, and showed her the original Clip Switch video uploaded by Vita, she at least stopped tutting and scoffing.

What really changed her mind was when they switched the television on in the kitchen. It was 7AM; the news had just started.

The mainstream media were finally catching up.

Sandra Lewis sat behind a desk. She was the morning anchor for ENTV, the right-leaning network owned by rich egotist Evers Nealy. It must have been the last thing Sarah had been watching, because she only turned the TV on as a distraction and didn't change the channel. They were all struggling to stay awake. In fact, Gina had dozed off several times.

"Chilling reports this morning from multiple parts of the country – and indeed the world – as multiple fatalities have occurred overnight, due to what some are claiming to be a mass online suicide pact targeted primarily at teens. Ninety-eight suspicious deaths have so far been recorded in the UK during the last forty-eight hours, many of them linked to the use of popular video-sharing app, Clip Switch. The social media giant is yet to comment, but is expected to make a statement later on today."

Shane bashed his fist on the table, startling Gina. "You see? I knew they would put a spin on it. A suicide pact? Really?"

Sarah folded her arms and paced around the kitchen. "You're telling me the news is lying? That they're just making it up?"

He rolled his eyes at her naivety. "Hard to believe, huh? They can't come out and say ghosts are real."

"Because they're not. They can't be."

"But they *are*," he told her for the umpteenth time.

"He's telling the truth, dear," said Gina supportively, clutching her bag on her lap. The glittery crucifix was back around her neck. "It takes some getting used to."

"I said the words," Shane admitted, and took a deep

breath. "Mandy has been visiting me. These scratches all over my face and arms are from her."

Sarah's neck bulged like she was going to be sick. If she were a cartoon character, she would've turned green. "Shane, if I find out any of this is a wind-up, I'll never forgive you."

"Do you think I would lie about Mandy?"

With a sigh, she shook her head. "No. No, I don't think you would. So, say I believe you. If Evie did this ritual, who would she have summoned? She's never lost anyone, unless you count our dog, Pogo, when she was eight."

Shane had loved that little cocker spaniel, and imagining it coming back from the grave, all twisted and snarling, was unpleasant. But he didn't think dead pets were involved in this. "I don't know the answer to that, Sarah, but Evie's in danger. We need to track her down right now."

"How? She won't answer her phone. She won't return my texts. There's no way she would allow us to get in this kind of state. I... I'm worried something has happened to her already."

Shane had been fearing the same thing. Evie was a teenager, which meant she was self-centred and dramatic by nature, but she wasn't a sociopath. There was no way she would send her family into a full-blown panic without even a text message to put their minds at ease.

"I have a guy in the police." Shane pulled out his mobile phone. The battery had been fighting to stay alive throughout the night, and it was currently only at nine per cent. "Let me make a call."

And so he did. He got in touch with his guy again, who

was thankfully awake and on his way to work. Although reticent, he agreed to help Shane when he said it concerned a missing family member. "This has got to stop. Just send me the details in a text," he said grumpily, and Shane did so immediately after ending the call.

Sarah looked at him. "What now?"

"We wait. It's not strictly legal, but my guy promised to locate Evie's phone as soon as he gets to the office. He's in Scotland Yard; he can get it done."

"How do you know a guy in Scotland Yard? From your days working at the newspaper?"

He nodded. "We go way back."

Gina was shaking her head in awe. "This friend of yours can tell us exactly where Evie is, just from her phone?"

"Providing it's switched on, yes. It's a contract phone, right?"

Sarah nodded. "With the amount it was costing me in top-ups, I had no choice."

"Okay, good, then we wait."

They returned their focus to the news. Sandra Lewis had been joined by a guest, a so-called 'tech guru' claiming that online terrorist groups were ramping up attacks on Western teenagers, coercing, manipulating, and blackmailing them into increasingly dangerous situations. This latest attack was likely down to a Russian hacking group named Kanzaza.

"What about the reports we've been getting about ghosts?" Sandra asked the spindly man in an oversized grey suit.

Shane perked up in his seat and paid closer attention.

He hadn't expected the media to address the truth directly, but they had.

Did you just go rogue, Sandra? Surely you wouldn't have been given the go-ahead by Evers Nealy to bring up ghosts on national news.

The guru shrugged petulantly. "Of course that's nonsense, and all part of the plot to distract us from the reality of what's actually going on. Vulnerable teens are being pressured into killing themselves, probably to avoid being blackmailed or extorted. Many of these teens expose themselves online, believing they're talking to young people of the same age. Those pictures are then used by criminals, who—"

"Yes, I understand that," said Sandra. "But there have apparently been multiple sightings of dead loved ones. In fact, reports are still coming in. How do you explain it? Is this some kind of mass hysteria?"

Shane nodded appreciatively. "Way to go, Sandra."

"Yes, I believe it is," said the guru. "If you tell people ghosts are real and repeat it enough times, eventually their minds will play tricks on them and they will believe it. It's also probably that these sightings are mere pranks. There's a silly ritual doing the rounds online, and it's been viewed millions of times. It makes sense that a few people are going to get carried away or frightened. One's mind goes back to the scary clown craze or bath salt zombies, doesn't it? The Internet has a way of bringing mischief-makers together."

"Indeed," said Sandra. "I'm glad you're able to put the nation's mind at ease. I think we can all agree that, if anything, recent events have highlighted a need for tougher

Internet restrictions, particularly where social media is concerned."

Shane groaned. "She's controlled opposition. Evers Nealy will probably use this entire thing as an excuse to kneecap his tech competitors."

"They can't deny this," said Gina. "It's too big. The truth will out. It always does."

"I hope you're right, but how bad do things have to get first?"

She clutched her crucifix and closed her eyes. "That is something I can't bear to think about."

Shane picked up his phone and sent a text to Ed.

Have you seen the news? I'm at my sister's. Evie is missing and I'm terrified. I really wish you were here.

Sarah stood up suddenly, making them both flinch. "I'm making toast," she said in a fraught tone. "Does anybody want toast?"

With empty stomachs, Gina and Shane both said yes.

CHAPTER FOURTEEN

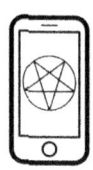

The text came through at eight forty-five. Shane's contact at the police station moved fast.

It was a simple text – just a postcode from an unknown number. The sender was being careful. Shane could appreciate that.

I need to stop calling on him. It's not right.

Shane got up out of his chair and bashed his knee on the table leg, but he didn't care. What was a little more pain? "I have an address."

Sarah was leaning against the counter, half-asleep, but she immediately straightened up. "Where?"

He told her the postcode, and then repeated it a second time when she pulled out her phone and searched for it. "Longman Street, Longman Street... Shane, that's not far from here. It's near the train station."

"I think I know it."

"Do you have the house number?"

He shook his head. "I don't think it's that accurate, but I'll knock on every door if I have to."

Sarah moved across the kitchen. "I'll get my coat."

"No!" He put up a hand. "Stay here in case Evie comes home. It's almost nine. She could catch a bus home."

"You think she will? I'll go crazy here by myself."

Shane went and put an arm around her. "I'll be as fast as I can, but we can't risk missing Evie if she comes home. Not if she's in danger."

"From ghosts?"

He nodded. "From ghosts. Trust me, okay?"

"I do. God knows why."

Gina stood up, clutching her bag. "I'd like to come. I can help knock on doors."

Shane thought she would be better off waiting with Sarah, but he had no right to tell her what to do. "Shouldn't you rest? You look ready to drop."

"I am, but I can't just go to sleep. Not yet. Let me help."

"Okay, but we need to hurry."

Sarah stood in the doorway as they headed out onto the driveway, too dazed to wave them off, but at least able to summon half a smile. Shane smiled back at her, then got in the car with Gina. He wasted no time switching on the engine, and he pulled away before they even got their seatbelts on.

They headed for the train station, only ten minutes away.

And Shane did something he hadn't done in a very long time. He prayed to God.

Please let her be okay.

Protect Evie.

Like you never protected Mandy.

. . .

When they reached the main road, something was off. It was the tail end of the early morning rush hour, yet traffic was light. Furthermore, several local shops – newsagents, garages, and hairdressers – still had their shutters lowered. The world hadn't woken up this morning.

Why?

Then it became obvious.

The first horror they encountered was a young man in his twenties scooting along the pavement on his butt, trying to get away from an old man swinging at his head with a walking stick. Black fumes billowed off the old man, while sticky entrails flapped behind him, looped around his belt. The lad screamed for dear life as the old man bashed his head in to a pulp.

The next attack was right around the corner – a pair of twin pre-teen girls in matching pink dresses skipping along a small football field, having fun. But instead of skipping ropes, they held what appeared to be bloody intestines. A dead body lay beneath a set of nearby goalposts, blood smeared all over the white-painted metal frame.

When they neared Longman Street, things got even worse.

People were running in and out of houses, or dashing into the middle of the road to flag down cars for help. It was difficult to distinguish the living from the dead, there was so much going on. Dogs barked furiously, clearly on the side of the living.

A girl sprinted out into the road and almost got hit by a bus, while a middle-aged man, completely naked, raced after her, his distended genitals flapping against his thighs.

A Rastafarian man stood on top of a white van,

clutching a young girl against his side while kicking out at an old black woman with tight white curls. She snatched at their ankles, trying to pull them down, but the man and girl were thankfully too quick for her. At first, the dead woman appeared to be in better shape than the other ghouls, but then she turned around and revealed a lopsided face, the obvious effects of a stroke.

They're all as they were in the moment of their deaths – naked in their beds, clutching their chests in the supermarket...

Drowning in a toddler's car seat.

"They're all coming back to attack their loved ones," said Shane, needing to keep his mind focused on finding answers, to keep himself from going insane. "Why?"

Even Creepy Krenshaw. He loved young girls, and that's who his victim was.

"There has to be a reason," said Gina. "I wish I'd devoted more of myself to learning after I left the convent, but I wanted to live my life."

"We'll figure this out."

They sped past a man hanging from a lamppost by his neck while a pale dead child hung from his legs and stretched him out. Gina groaned, clouding up the passenger window with her breath. "Things'll never be the same after this."

It was undeniably true, but a part of Shane wondered if that might be a good thing. Perhaps the dead returning was the slap in the face mankind needed. The cataclysmic event to shift things back into perspective.

Our souls matter. Our actions matter.

A Labrador raced across the road, howling. Shane yanked the wheel to avoid it.

Mandy appeared in the centre of the road, a flickering shadow, a smoking black veil. Her eyes met his.

"Shit!" Shane yanked the wheel again, this time harder.

The steering went light.

The road tilted.

And the Land Cruiser tipped over onto its side. It skidded across the potholed road and leapt the kerb up onto the pavement. Shane screamed a silent scream. Gina yelled for dear life.

Time seemed to slow down.

Noise amplified – metal scraping against concrete. A symphony of chaos.

Then the entire world imploded as a colossal impact rattled Shane's bones and glass rained down all over him.

All was still. All was quiet.

All was pain.

"Fuck me," said Gina.

Shane knew he was horizontal from the pressure inside his skull. All the blood was rushing to the right side of his face, and when he turned his head, he saw the road right outside his window. A cold breeze rushed in through the space where once there had been a windscreen.

Gina was lying across his lap, her head inches from the inside of the driver's side door. Her auburn hair was dark and wet in places, stained with blood. Panicked, he grabbed her shoulders and shook her. "Gina? Gina, speak to me?"

To his relief, she let out a weak moan. "Am I dead?"

"No. No, you're okay."

"What happened?"

"I think I'm finally going to have to get a new car. We crashed. I swerved."

Mandy was here.

Gina lifted her head from his leg but then began to slide downwards. After leaving Sarah's in a hurry, neither of them had put on their seatbelts.

"I don't think anything's broken," said Gina, but then she hissed in pain. "I might be wrong."

Shane grabbed her so that she wouldn't slide any more, and then, with great effort, managed to lower her down against the bottom of the car. From there, she could look at him. A thick gash bled on her forehead. "You're bleeding," he said. "We need to get you some help."

"No. Go and find Evie. We're almost there."

She was right. Longman Street was close by. He could walk it, so long as his legs weren't a total mess.

Testing out his limbs, one by one, he became fairly certain he had escaped the crash with only scrapes and bruises. The Land Cruiser had taken most of the damage. But that damage was terminal.

Thank you for your service.

With a groan, Shane tried to shift himself out of the tangle he was in with Gina. They were both slumped at the bottom of the car, which was actually the driver's side lying against the road. To get out, he would need to climb up through the passenger door, or out through the missing windscreen. Through the various gaps, he could see people rushing back and forth in the street, but no one came to help. They were too busy screaming in terror at their own torment.

Ghosts. They're everywhere.

"I need to get help," he said again, and reached into his pocket. It was awkward to manoeuvre, but he managed to slide his phone out. The battery was dead. "Damn, I can't make a call."

"Forget help," said Gina. "Like you said before, it's just us. And your niece needs you. Go! I'll be fine. Someone'll come, eventually."

Shane listened to more screaming and didn't feel confident at all that help would ever come. But he had to help Evie. "I'll call someone as soon as I can, Gina. I won't leave you stuck in here like this."

"Eh, I can use the rest. I'll just lie here for a bit."

He chuckled, tasting blood in his mouth. "Thank you."

"For dragging you into this mess?"

"For sticking with me through all this, and for giving a shit about me."

"My pleasure. Now hurry up. I'm getting claustrophobic with you lying on top of me."

"Right." With a heave, Shane shifted himself around. His legs got caught up against the seat, so he used his hands to pull himself into position. Trying not to squash Gina, he shuffled on his side towards the open windscreen. Shards of broken glass bit into his skin, but thankfully they were thick chunks rather than flesh-slicing teeth. The pain was uncomfortable, but the actual damage was minimal. He took the worst of it on his elbow.

"Good luck, Shane. I-I hope you find her."

"I will," he said, dragging himself out onto the road. "I'm going to find her."

The sunshine was overwhelmingly bright as he pulled himself out of the car, and he had to blink several times to get the blurriness out of his eyes. Standing up was a chore, and both legs shook like he'd just run a marathon. His knees produced an unhealthy clicking sound.

But he made it to his feet.

The first thing he did was turn around to examine his trusty Land Cruiser.

The 4x4 was on its side, bodywork crushed inwards. The wheels still spun, slowly, and shards of glass and plastic littered the road all around it.

Something trickled down the middle of the chassis. Shane took a moment to identify it, making sure it was only oil and not petrol. The last thing he wanted was to come back and find Gina burnt to a crisp.

"Are you okay in there?"

"Yes, I'm fine. Will you just – ah!"

"What is it?"

She let out an irritable grunt. "It's nothing. I leant on something. It's fine. Go on, won't you!"

"It doesn't feel right leaving you."

"If the Lord wanted me dead, I would be."

"Okay, I'll... I'll be back as soon as I can." He turned around, fighting the urge to stay with Gina and try to get her out. But, at her age, it was probably better to wait for trained help. Who knew what damage she could do to her elderly bones if she tried to move?

He had to go. Evie needed him.

Putting one foot in front of the other, Shane got

moving. There was chaos all around, but it quickly became part of the background. He saw screaming victims and nightmarish ghosts, but his mind was focused only on getting to Longman Street.

Focused on his niece who needed him.

I wasn't there when Mandy and Emily drowned.

But I'm going to be there for you, Evie.

He was too beat to run, even to jog, but he walked briskly, trying to keep his balance as his knees and thighs spasmed and tried to betray him.

How much can you push your body before it just gives up?

Can you have a heart attack at thirty-nine?

There was a dog up ahead, standing on the grassy verge beside the road. Some kind of golden spaniel. Its hackles were raised all along its spine, and its droopy ears were pinned back. When it saw Shane coming, it started to bark.

"Hey," said Shane. "I'm not a ghost. Chill out."

But the dog didn't chill out. It barked at him furiously, hopping back and forth.

Shane wasn't fearful of dogs, but he slowed right down to be cautious. The dog was acting like a lunatic. Had its mind broken due to what was going on? What on earth did dogs make of the dead returning?

Shane put out a hand and approached the dog carefully. He still had to make it to Evie, and he wasn't going to let a spaniel stand in his way. "Easy there, boy. I'm just trying to get past."

The dog stopped barking and began to growl. It lowered down on its haunches, teeth bared, lips pulled back.

"What is your problem? Why are you growling at—" Shane paused, a strange sensation washing over him. Slowly, he realised the dog wasn't growling at *him* at all.

It's growling at something right behind me.

Shane spun around as quickly as he could.

Mandy reached out and grabbed the bottom of his shirt with a chubby, clenched fist. "Dah."

Shane lost his balance, going down onto one knee. Mandy swiped at his face like a cat, but he reared back and avoided her jagged nails. He tried to get back to his feet, but she held him down by a fistful of shirt.

"Mandy, let go of me!"

"Abba. Dah!"

Shane heard the word Abba clearly and knew what his dead daughter was saying. *Abba* was another word for God. Gina had been right. The agony of being torn away from Heaven was what turned the dead angry. The grief of it sent them insane.

"You'll be back with him soon, sweetie. I promise."

Instead of attacking again, Mandy tilted her head. For a moment, the dark unknowableness in her eyes shifted, letting through a slither of light – of life. "Dah."

"I love you, Mandy. I really wish we'd got to know each other."

The darkness returned. The little dead girl snarled.

Shane used both hands to push her away, to unhook her from his shirt, but she was too strong. It wasn't until the spaniel leapt at her from the side that she finally let go of him.

He staggered down the road, listening to the spaniel yelping and his daughter hiss, but he couldn't bring himself to turn around and absorb whatever carnage was happening behind him.

Thanks, Fido. I owe you one.

He walked, picking up speed as he hurried towards Longman Street.

I love you, Mandy. But I have to focus on the living.

CHAPTER FIFTEEN

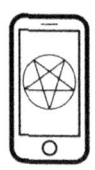

Shane was limping by the time he made it to his destination. Redlake train station was three hundred metres behind him, along with the Railway Inn that was unanimously agreed upon to be the roughest pub in town. Nearby Longman Street was an undesirable place to live.

The houses here were narrow mid-century terraces, the kind with extra-long gardens meant for post-war allotments. They were in various states of upkeep, some having brand-new composite doors and windows in fashionable grey, while others had rotting wooden frames decades old. Others had council-issue PVC. It was either a postcode on the up, or one on the down. Only the residents would truly know.

The air was alive with sirens – ambulance, fire brigade, and police cars – the crisis trifecta. Shit was going down, and Shane once again felt utterly powerless. He'd known how bad things were long before everybody else, but he hadn't been able to do a damn thing about it.

Even now, ghosts roamed the streets, stalking their prey.

Up ahead, a young woman hung by her fingertips from a bedroom window, trying to escape an old crone with hair tied up in a dirty hairnet. Before Shane could get near, the crone smashed the woman's hands and caused her to fall. The height alone wouldn't have killed her, but she landed awkwardly and went stumbling backwards, where she fell and smashed the base of her skull on a brick wall surrounding the front garden. The meaty crack left no ambiguity. The woman was dead.

From the bedroom window, the old crone cackled.

In front of another house, a man in a white shirt and a red tie stood shoulder to shoulder with a much larger man. The two of them held cricket bats and were beating at a young woman who was wearing a blue supermarket shirt and no trousers. Every time they beat at her, she rose back up like a zombie. She even moaned hungrily like one. Her original cause of death obviously had something to do with the massive hole right through the middle of her torso. Shane could see right through her.

None of this horror bothered him, however. What upset him most was what followed behind him.

Since passing the Railway Inn, Shane had been glancing back every few metres. Each time, he saw Mandy in the distance, toddling after him like an implacable dread. His only mercy was that she seemed unable to catch up with him, remaining the same distance behind the entire time, popping in and out of sight as she moved behind cars and buildings.

All he could do was concentrate on going forward.

He reached the entrance to Longman Street and was relieved to find it a relatively small cul-de-sac of perhaps thirty houses. It wouldn't take long to knock on every door.

Was his niece in one of these properties?

I'm going to find you, Evie.

Best I get started.

He limped over to the nearest house, which turned out to be number thirteen. Not a great number to start with, but his luck couldn't get much worse.

Bad luck? Ha, I never would have even believed in bad luck before this started. Now, I'm ready to believe in anything. Witches, zombies, demons from Hell? Yep, it all seems perfectly reasonable now.

He knocked on the door, but no one answered. Needing to do something other than simply walk away, he beat on the door with his fists and yelled out Evie's name as loudly as he could.

Then he went to number twelve and did the same. At this house, someone hung out of the top window and told him to go away. It was a middle-aged man dressed in a black security uniform – possibly a bailiff or court enforcement officer. He'd obviously been getting ready for work that morning before things had turned crazy. From how freaked out he looked, Shane had no reason to believe he knew Evie's whereabouts.

"Come on, Evie. Where are you?"

He tried number eleven and number ten and number nine, but no one was answering. They were either at work, or off somewhere dealing with their own problems. Every time he beat on the front doors, he yelled out Evie's name.

By the time he reached house number six, Mandy had

entered the close. She staggered back and forth unsteadily, her yellow onesie filthy with so much blood that it almost looked black. Shane had a sinking feeling the blood belonged to the spaniel.

Because surely the dead don't bleed.

He was running out of time. If Mandy caught up to him, he wasn't sure he had the strength to fight her off. This was it, the end. The last of his strength remained, and he needed to make it count.

"Evie! Where the fuck are you?"

"Hey? Hey, over here!"

Shane's eyes had been fixed on Mandy, shambling ever closer, so it took several seconds of the stranger calling out before he finally turned around to see who it was.

He saw a young lad standing out in the front garden of a house on the opposite side of the road. His floppy brown hair was shaved at the sides, and he wore a pair of godawful skinny jeans. He was calling out to Shane, a desperate look in his eye.

"Who are you?" Shane demanded.

"I heard you shouting. Are you... are you looking for Evie? Evie Mogg?"

Shane took a step into the road, painfully aware that Mandy was gaining on him, but he needed to know who this young lad was. "Do you know where she is?"

"S-she's inside. She..." He shook his head, close to tears. "It's fucked up, man."

"What's fucked up?" Shane took another few steps, almost falling down, but held up by rage and urgency. "Tell me what's happened to my niece right now or you'll never take another breath."

"I can't explain it. Please, just come with me." The lad turned and dashed towards the house.

Shane found the energy to run after him.

The house Shane entered was one of the more run-down properties on Longman Street. Its front lawn was littered with empty energy drink cans and greasy KFC buckets. The wooden door number – twenty-three – was chipped and peeling, and the lantern beside the front door was missing a bulb. The front door hung wide open.

The young lad was standing on the doorstep, frantic. He pulled Shane inside the hallway and almost fell down from exertion. His white T-shirt was badly stained, his face pale and sweaty.

Shane nodded to him. "Hey, kid, you're bleeding."

"It don't matter. Just help Evie."

The lad needed help, but Shane didn't care about that right now. "Where is she?"

"She... she's locked in the bathroom."

Shane got in the lad's face, forcing him back against the wall. "I swear, if you did anything to hurt her..."

His eyes almost popped out of his head as he cowered before Shane. "I swear, man, I would never hurt Evie. It's..." He shook his head, bottom lip quivering. "You won't fucking believe me. It's too crazy."

Shane wobbled as he tried to maintain his firm demeanour. Truthfully, the kid could probably knock him on his arse even with an injury. "Try me."

"There's this old woman in the house, man. She's trying to kill Evie. I... I tried to stop her, but..." He clutched his bleeding stomach and groaned. "She tore me apart, man. All I could do was shove Evie into the bathroom and lock the door before the old bitch tossed me down the stairs. When I came to, I heard you shouting. I... I'm Tommy, by the way."

"Her boyfriend, I'm assuming?"

"Yeah. It's Shane, right? Evie always says how cool you are."

"You and I aren't starting off on the right foot, kid, trust me. How long have you been seeing my niece?"

"A-about four months. I really care about her, man. She's the most amaz—"

"Just show me where she is."

"Yeah, okay, follow me." He staggered down the hallway, looking around sheepishly, clearly afraid but pushing through it. At the end of the space, he opened a door and stepped though into a cramped dining room, where he revealed a staircase behind a second door. "Bathroom's up there. I... I can't go up again, man. I'm... I'm..."

Shane saw the kid was struggling just to stay standing, so he grabbed him and manoeuvred him onto a wooden chair placed around a cheap pine dining table. "Sit down and try to breathe slowly. You're going to bleed out faster if you're panicking."

The kid began to cry – and that was all he was, a kid. Shane put his anger aside for a moment and wrapped an arm around him. "I'm going to get you some help, Tommy. You're going to be okay. Just put pressure on the wound and try to stay calm for me."

"I'm sorry. She's up there all alone. I should have—"

"Let me handle it."

"She's dead, man."

Shane's blood turned to ice. "What?"

"The old woman upstairs. She's dead. I swear."

Relieved, Shane nodded. "I know. It's happening everywhere."

"W-what?"

"The world's gone a little crazy. Imagine Wes Craven took over the reins of existence. That's kind of where we're at."

"Who?"

"Never mind." Shane stepped over to the door and nudged it all the way open. The staircase inside looped around a corner, heading upwards and creating a small footprint, as was the case with many narrow homes like this.

The very first step creaked so loudly Shane thought someone was yelling at him, and it caused him to freeze. The wooden board flexed beneath his foot, and he wondered how long ago it had been nailed in place. This house was like a ghost itself, built by the hands of men who were probably all dead now. Families come and gone. Years rolled by, society ever-changing, but not this staircase. This staircase was older than he was.

But it was what was at the top of the stairs that really concerned him.

An old woman is trying to kill Evie? Who?

Who did she bring back from the dead?

Shane climbed slowly to the top of the stairs, holding onto the bannister to keep from plummeting backwards. The carpet on the landing was threadbare, the skirting boards in need of painting. Was this Tommy's house? His parents'?

How much time has Evie been spending here?

"Ssson!"

All questions left Shane's head, replaced by utter incomprehension as he stared down the landing at a woman who had once meant the world to him, but who also haunted his nightmares. A woman responsible for so much of who he was.

Shane shook his head in disbelief. "M-Mother?"

CHAPTER SIXTEEN

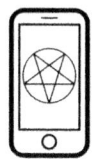

Shane's mother glared at him from across the landing. Her jowls sagged worse than they ever had in life, and her once green eyes were now the deepest black. She wore a smart knee-length skirt and sensible black heels, as well as a silky cream blouse. It had been one of her favourite outfits; the one she'd been wearing on the evening she had suffered a heart attack and fallen down the stairs. The flesh around her throat was folded and stretched from where she'd broken her neck. "Ssson…" she said again, hissing like a pit viper.

Shane put a hand on the wall to steady himself. "Why are you here? Evie never even knew you."

"Graaaaandaughter. Fatherless bastard!"

Shane shook his head and sneered. "Hell hasn't changed you, I see? How's the weather down there?"

Black fumes billowed from her rounded shoulders in response to his insolence. Her eyes swirled, two portals into the abyss. Her tongue flicked between her crusted lips as she spat out chunks of decaying, fleshy spittle. "It burns."

Shane nodded. His mind crowded with emotions. This woman had made his life an utter misery, and yet she had been miserable too. Her psyche had been a barren, inhospitable place, but she had been forced to live there. How much could you blame a sick person for their actions?

"I'm sorry, Mother. I'm sorry you've been in a bad place, but you need to go back there. I won't let you hurt Evie."

"Silence!" She floated across the landing, a billowing black cloud in the shape of a rotting corpse.

"What are you?" Shane demanded, standing his ground. "Is my mother truly in there?"

The phantom came to a stop, inches from his face. The visage of his mother snarled, the stench of her wicked and foul. "I'm here, son. I see what you are. A sinner. You are weak."

"No. I did everything you asked."

"Weak!" A tendril of black smoke lashed out across his cheek. It filled him with a cold dread, an icy fist around his heart.

My father's weak heart.

Shane fell to the carpet, clutching his now bleeding cheek. "Stop! Mother!"

"You offended God. Your sins sent me to Hell." She whipped at him again, drawing more blood from the side of his head. "Your weakness tarnishes my soul. Drinking, fornication, BLASPHEMY!"

Shane wailed as the darkness whipped at him again and again. The pain was so immense that he didn't even know where it came from. All he could do was cover up and beg for it to end. "I was a good boy. I did what you told me."

"Your mind is full of sin. It's you who should burn. You who should suffer in the inferno that houses the wicked."

"No. No, I'm good."

"Sinner!"

"Uncle Shane?" It was Evie. Her voice came through the door at the end of the landing. "Is that you?"

Shane couldn't catch his breath from screaming. The old familiar agony in his knees began to bloom – hundreds of imagined grains of rice digging into his delicate cartilage. He was a child again. Powerless. Worthless.

No. I'm an uncle and a brother.

A husband and a dad. I'll never stop being a dad.

Shane absorbed the blows that rained down on him and got to his feet. "E-Evie? I'm here."

"Uncle Shane! Please, help me."

He straightened up to face his mother. "Leave her alone."

"She is mine." She whipped around like a black velvet sheet and then rushed towards the bathroom door. The woodwork was already battered and splintered, and it began to split even more as she whipped sharp, smokey daggers against it. It wouldn't be long before she made it inside. Evie knew it too because she screamed at the top of her lungs.

"Bastard child. You shall burn in Hell."

Shane took a step forward, planted his feet firmly enough to trust them. "Leave her alone, you bitch!"

His mother froze in front of the door. The black smoke

around her flickered ever so slightly, but she was almost completely still. She began to turn around slowly.

He'd never spoken back to her before. Never told her what he really thought of her.

Time to stop being an honourable son.

What faced Shane was a creature of intolerable spite. The dead were not returning as they were, only an echo of a person mixed with something foul and obscene. He saw that now. Perhaps Nomon's Ritual didn't work the way it had used to for those Sicilian monks in the seventies.

His mother glared at him in a baleful manner she had never possessed in life. A hissing sound surrounded her, like searing bacon. "I will drag you into the inferno where we can be together forever."

Shane swallowed a lump in his throat. "I... I'm glad you're dead. My only regret is that you ever lived in the first place. You tortured Sarah and me. You broke our minds and shattered our spirits. Despite that, we survived you. We made lives for ourselves. Sarah's a loving mother, something you could never understand, and I was a good father and a decent husband. We beat you, Mother. Sarah and I didn't let your wickedness infect us. It's a miracle."

"Transgressor!" She rushed towards him, a howling black wind.

"It's time for you to leave! It's time for you—"

Shane left his feet as a colossal force struck his chest and sent him hurtling backwards. He anticipated a painful landing on the floor, but his fall continued, his body rotating backwards. His heart stopped beating.

He crashed down on the stairs – ribs cracking – and proceeded to tumble head over heels down and around the corner. Gravity spat him out at the bottom of the stairs and violently deposited him onto the dining room's hard wooden floor.

Tommy was still somewhere in the room, because Shane heard him cry out. He couldn't see the lad, however, as everything had gone black. He was blind. His body shattered, his brain damaged.

M-my heart.

It started beating.

He groaned.

I'm not dying.

No... not today.

Slowly, his vision returned. At first blurry, but then clear. He tested his limbs. They moved sluggishly.

Tommy appeared beside him, white as a sheet. "Sh-Shane? Are you all right?"

"No. G-get help."

The lad nodded and raced off without question.

Shane lay on his back, taking in painful breaths. He'd never really been injured before, and it terrified him to know he was broken in multiple places. At the same time, he was too tired to panic.

The staircase door crashed against the wall.

Shane couldn't move.

His mother appeared, flowing over and around him.

Life flashed in front of Shane. Memories of him and Sarah hiding out in the garden, pretending they were invisible fairies while their mother yelled in search of them. Memories of her sneaking into his bed late at night, sobbing because their mother had taken away her duvet and forced her to shiver, unclothed on her mattress.

Memories of Sarah leaving him with their mother alone.

And him not being brave enough to go with her.

Evie being born. Him being there at the birth. The only family Sarah had.

I'm not alone.

I didn't lose everybody.

"Burn," said his mother. "Burn with me."

"You... you're not my mother. You're just the worst parts of her shaped into something hideous. Wherever she really is, Heaven or Hell, I forgive her."

"Forgiveness is beyond you."

"N-no... My mother was ill. She went through life trapped in a private nightmare. It's time..." He faded for a moment, his head swimming. He clenched his jaw and brought himself back into focus. "It's time I stopped blaming her. Life sucks, but I can try to make my little part of it better."

Giving a dying speech to a hate-filled revenant was not how he'd seen his life ending, but he was strangely at peace with it. His only regret was the fate of his niece. Evie was innocent. It was his job to protect her.

But I'm broken. I can't move.

The black cloud thickened around him, blotting out everything else. He might have already been dead, but the pain in his bones told him otherwise. "Forgive me," he said, thinking of Evie, his sister, and everyone else who had ever tried to get close to him. "Forgive me."

The darkness washed over him, filling his head with the most terrible of shrieks. He felt needles on his skin, pressure in his chest. The darkness reached inside him, wrapped itself around his struggling heart.

He heard the voices of his friends, a final comfort at the end.

"Holy shit!" said Ed.

"*In nomine Patris, et Filii, et Spiritus Sancti,*" said a tired voice he was certain belonged to Gina. "Be gone with you!"

Shane opened his eyes but still saw only darkness. His heart spluttered painfully in his chest. His breathing came rapidly.

I hear them. Gina and Ed.

How?

"Shane?" said Ed's voice again. "Shane, we're here."

The darkness receded, letting out more inhuman shrieks. It was recoiling. Shrinking.

Retreating.

Slowly, the world returned. Shane got a peek of Ed, standing in the dining room. Then he saw Gina, standing with her glittering crucifix. She was chanting in Latin, words he didn't understand.

The visage of his mother evaporated, leaving behind a layer of black ash over everything, and a smell so foul it made everyone's eyes water.

Shane remained on his back, unable to move. Gina, Ed, and Tommy looked down at him.

"E-Evie," he said. "Help Evie."

Then he passed out.

. . .

Rather than immediately help Evie, Ed and Tommy helped Shane to his feet as he regained consciousness. Surprisingly, he was able to hold himself up, although he was bleeding all over and could barely catch his breath.

He moved over to the staircase door. "She's up there. We need to go get her."

Ed reached out and grabbed him as he lost his balance. "We will. Take it easy. We've got you."

His head fell, but he managed to look at her. "H-how are you here?"

"You left a message. I went to your sister's house and she told me where you were. Tommy was out in the garden calling for help. So I came."

He shook his head. "And Gina?"

"Wandering along the side of the road like a zombie. I picked her up in my car and she told me everything."

"As much as I had time for," said Gina. The side of her face was caked in blood from the gash on her forehead. She appeared dangerously frail. The crucifix was shaking in her hand. "Are you okay, Mr Mogg?"

He turned to Tommy. "You have a Bible in this house?"

"W-why would I have a Bible?"

He shook his head and sighed. "Do you have a phone then?"

"Yeah, of course." He reached into his pocket and handed it over. "Why?"

"Because it's not over," he said. "This whole thing isn't over. What's your PIN?"

Tommy gave it to him and then asked, "What's happening? Outside…"

Gina did the sign of the cross. "It's like the end times out there."

"It's bad," said Ed. "Real bad."

Shane nodded. "It's not the dead returning. It's something else." He turned to Gina. "We need God on our side, right?"

"Always. What are you planning to do?"

"I'm going to have faith."

Before anyone could speak, he started up the stairs. He knew they would follow, but he needed to do this himself. He needed to be the one to reach Evie and make her safe. It was his job. He was her uncle.

It took great effort to make it to the landing, and he needed to use his hands to make it up the final steps. At the top, he had to lean on the wall and slide himself along, leaving bloody smears on the paintwork as he moved towards the battered bathroom door.

Evie sobbed inside.

"I'm here," he said. "It's okay."

"Uncle Shane? I'm so sorry. I did this."

"No. None of this is your fault. You're a good kid."

"I'm not. I... I'm not."

He made it to the door and slumped against it, his forehead pressed against the sharp, splintered wood. "I love you. So does your mum. You're loved."

She sobbed louder. "Who is she? W-why does she want to hurt me?"

"I don't know the answer to that, Evie, but she's gone. I'm going to keep you safe." He squeezed the phone in his hand, reminding himself he still had it. "Open the door."

She didn't seem to move on the other side.

"Evie, it's okay. Let me in."

"I'm pregnant."

He smiled. "I know. We all know, you muppet."

She gasped. "Mum is gonna kill me."

"You just got attacked by the ghost of my dead mother. You want to have this conversation now?"

"No. No, I suppose not. Wait, your mother?"

"Yeah. I'm glad you two finally got to meet. What do you think?"

"She's a mad bitch."

"You don't know the half of it. Open up now, Evie. I'm here."

There was a shuffling sound, and the door handle turned. The door was so battered that it dragged along the carpet as she pulled it, and Shane had to help get it fully open.

Gina appeared on the stairs behind him, but she kept her distance. Ed must have been downstairs, trying to keep Tommy from dying of his gut wound.

She came back. I needed help and she was here for me.

She's my friend.

The sight of Evie was like a miracle. She was unharmed, despite the tears on her face. He wrapped his arms around her and breathed her in. "Thank God you're okay."

"You don't believe in God," she said, her voice thick and phlegmy.

"Eh, it's complicated."

The room went cold.

Shane had his face buried in Evie's ginger hair, but he raised his eyes to look behind her.

The sunlight coming through the frosted-glass window slowly blotted out, a shadowy eclipse emerging from nowhere.

His mother returned, materialising inside the bathroom.

Shane grabbed his niece and threw her behind him, just as the darkness lashed out.

"Go!"

Evie screamed. "Shane!"

"Go!"

Shane took a slice on the arm, but stood his ground, desperate to keep the wickedness from chasing his niece.

But the darkness knocked him aside like a child.

It flowed down the landing, snatching Evie by her hair and lifting her up. She screamed at the top of her lungs.

Gina tried to confront the evil with her crucifix, but it lashed out and knocked the old woman down. The black cloud was spitting and hissing, slithers of shadow drifting away from it as though it were struggling to keep itself together.

"Burn," came a raspy voice. The darkness no longer resembled Shane's mother. It was just an evil, all-consuming blackness, a complete absence of existence.

And it wants Evie.

Shane lifted the phone, entered the PIN, and opened up the browser. He entered the words '*Lord's Prayer*' and hit search. Familiar words came up, ones he knew almost perfectly.

But it's been a while and I don't want to forget.

As Evie screamed and Gina moaned, Shane marched down the landing with the phone held out in front of himself. "Our Father, who art in Heaven, hallowed be thy name; thy kingdom come; thy will be done; on earth as it is in Heaven." He tossed the phone aside. He didn't need it. "Give us this day our daily bread. And forgive us our trespasses, as we forgive those who trespass against us."

The darkness swirled, evaporating more and more. It had Evie around the throat and she was gagging and turning blue.

"And lead us not into temptation; but deliver us from evil."

A black hurricane formed on the landing. The pressure released itself from Evie's throat. She crumpled to the ground, gasping.

Shane threw out an arm. "Run! Get out of the house."

Evie's eyes bulged as she looked at him, and for a moment it looked like she was going to refuse to leave him. But then she clambered to her feet and raced down the stairs. Gina had propped herself up against the wall and was clutching her chest.

The darkness flowed around Shane again. He felt his flesh pulling away from his bones, the evil trying to tear him apart.

But he was ready to finish this.

At the top of his lungs, he shouted, "For thine is the kingdom, the power and the glory, for ev—"

Something lashed out of the darkness.

Shane's neck suddenly turned cold as the air left his lungs. He clamped a hand against the left side of his jaw and felt hot blood gushing between his fingers. He tried to speak, but his throat seized up. His legs buckled.

As he hit the ground, he knew it was over.

The darkness spread out around him, ready to pull him into an empty, soulless place.

"For ever and ever," said Gina in gasping voice. "Amen."

The black cloud came apart like dust in a fan, reduced to the smallest molecules within a split second before disappearing. It made no sound, gave off no threats. It was just gone.

Gina crawled along the carpet towards Shane.

Then she began to cry out for help.

"It's okay, Mr Mogg. I'm here. I won't leave you."

"Thank you," he managed to say, before he passed out from the blood loss.

Shane woke up in the hospital. He was alone, until he pressed a buzzer and a nurse came. She checked his vitals and told him he was lucky to be alive. Then she rushed off in a panic. He had a feeling he wasn't the only person close to death today. In fact, the hospital sounded chaotic.

Ed arrived half an hour later, looking exhausted, her pink hair caked in dust and grime. But she had the most wonderful of smiles for him. "I swear, if you had died on me, I would've done the ritual and brought you back just to give you hell."

He moaned, the vibration causing his neck to ache. "Don't joke. How long have I been here?"

"They brought you in about six hours ago. You've had surgery. They'll probably move you to a ward soon."

"My throat was cut?"

"Actually, it was your jugular. I raced you to the

hospital myself while Tommy squeezed your neck and tried to stop the blood."

"Tommy?" He shook his head as he reminded himself who the lad even was. "He and I have a conversation ahead of us."

"Go easy on him. He's just a kid."

Shane nodded. From what he'd seen of Tommy, the kid at least seemed to care about Evie, and he had stuck around when he could easily have made a run for it.

Kid still got my sixteen-year-old niece pregnant though. He's not going to be getting away with that lightly.

"Where's Gina? Evie?"

"Evie's in the waiting room with her mum. Gina's in another hospital bed somewhere around here. She's got broken ribs and a concussion. That old chick is tough."

"You have no idea."

"She told me about Mandy. I'm sorry I wasn't there. I was ignoring your messages because of everything that happened, and I was just in a bad headspace after getting locked out of my place."

"Don't be sorry. I was a bad friend. You're my favourite person in the whole world, and there's a bedroom waiting for you at my house."

She smirked. "You sure? I'm kind of messy."

"Hello, have you met me? Yeah, I'm sure. I'm tired of being alone. Come and stay with me. It'll be fun."

"We can be alone together."

"Sounds like a plan. I can't believe you turned up when you did. Did you not go to your parents?"

"I did." She sat down on the end of his bed. "But I headed back when I heard you apologise in one of your voicemails. I knew then that something must have been really wrong."

"I'm sorry," he said without difficulty. "I'm really, really sorry."

"I don't even know what you're apologising for, but you're forgiven. You're not as bad as you think, Shane."

He turned his head, and a tear slid down his cheek onto his pillow. "I've been doing sketchy shit for far too long."

"What do you mean?" She frowned. "Shane?"

"You know how you're always wondering how I got so many contacts?"

"Yeah, so what?"

"It's blackmail. I blackmail people, Ed. Been doing it for years."

"You're shitting me? You write articles about alien abduction and Avril Lavigne clone conspiracies. What exactly are you blackmailing people about?"

"It was more from my time before I joined *Splatt!*"

"When you worked for one of the big rags?" She shrugged and looked away. "I suppose that's the name of the game in mainstream media, right?"

"No. Actually it's the reason I got fired. I didn't do it to get stories and help my career, I did it because I was angry. After Em and Mandy died, I wanted the joyriding kids brought to justice. But the police ballsed up the investigation. They never found who did it. The officer in charge of the investigation was the first person I blackmailed. I caught him visiting a brothel and videoed him. I threatened to show his wife and explode his life unless he did me favours when I needed them."

"Jesus, Shane."

"I know. Anger is a hell of a thing. Anyway, after I joined *Splatt!* I toned things down, but I still have dirt on various people and use it when I need it. So many people have been living on edge because of the situations I've forced them into. I'm a bad person, Ed."

"So, what are you going to do about it?"

"Fix it. End it. Fess up."

"Forget that! Stop blackmailing people, of course, but don't punish yourself. What good will that do? Just be better. Be the good bloke I know you are deep down. Show me the man you were before life took a great big dump on you."

He tried to smile but couldn't. "How bad is it? Out there?"

"It's a shit show. The news is reporting it as some kind of atmospheric gas, causing illusions and erratic behaviour. They're not mentioning the word ghosts at all. Kids are getting hurt all over though. The hospital is overrun. It's bad."

"We need to stop it."

"We will."

Shane shook his head, barely able to feel his body beneath the clean white sheets. "How? How do we stop it?"

"Same way you got rid of your psycho mum. People need to start exorcising their ghosts. Figure out a way we can make that happen and we have a chance of controlling this."

"My mother's really gone?"

Ed shrugged. "She hasn't come after Evie again. All the

signs are good. Looks like English is as good as Latin. Gina told me about the Lord's Prayer. How did you know?"

"I didn't. But I've seen crucifixes and holy water do the trick, so why not prayer? That thing trying to hurt Evie was unholy, so it makes sense."

"Ironic, considering how religious your mum was in life."

"It wasn't really her," he said. "It was like the worst parts of her. She was a tyrant, but she had good traits too – a whole personality. She used to love singing, cooking... Sometimes, when she was in a good place, she would play board games with us. We had fun. All of that was missing, though, when I looked into her eyes. I saw only madness and judgement and anger."

Ed nodded. "The bad bits?"

"I wish I could understand it." He clenched his jaw and endured a wave of pain that washed over him. He gripped the bedsheets.

"You okay?"

He gasped. "Just a bit broken, but I'll live."

"Good to hear."

"We need to find Vita," he said. "He's responsible for this. He can't get away with it."

She smiled. "Yeah, about that. There's another reason I came racing back, besides your whiny voicemails. My guy, the one I sent the video to? He came back to me. I know exactly where Vita is."

Despite the agony, Shane managed to sit up in bed.

CHAPTER 17

Shane couldn't believe this had all fallen upon him and Ed. Even if they called the police, nothing would happen. No crime had technically been committed, and even if there had been, any prosecution would involve admitting the Clip Switch massacre had been caused by ghosts.

Of course, that wasn't the narrative being spun by any of the big news outlets. During the last four days, anyone claiming a ghost had killed a member of their family had been dismissed as grief-sick at best, or deranged conspiracy theorists at worst. No, the teen death toll had been caused by subliminal messages in a spate of strange online videos – all of which had now been deleted from Clip Switch's servers by a mysterious hacking group. Mass hallucinations and suicidal impulses were the hot topics of the day.

Alongside freedom of the Internet.

Evers Nealy and other tech moguls were piling on the pressure, lobbying to have the Chinese Clip Switch app banned outright. Outraged parents and slimy politicians were all too happy to jump on the bandwagon. A bill was being brought before Parliament to classify social media as an adult-only service, the same as gambling. Shane didn't really care about any of that.

He cared about the monster who was truly responsible for the deaths of Stefani, Hannah, Jess, Millie, and countless others. The man who had put Nomon's Ritual online.

Vita.

It had been exactly one week since Shane had sat down and received that first email from Jester. Seven days to finally get the answers he needed.

Why would somebody do this?

Ed's phone chirped, and she pulled it from the pocket of her denim jacket. "Huh," she said with a smile. "Evie's posted another video."

Shane leant over, clutching his sore ribs, and looked at her screen. On it, Evie was performing a short Latin prayer that Gina had written down while in a hospital bed. It was an exorcism of sorts, with the ability to dispel the darkness. Several of Evie's videos had gone viral, and kids all over the Internet owed their lives to her for helping them get rid of their ghosts. She already had over three million adoring followers. Hopefully, the new ritual would continue to spread, and the crisis would all be over.

"She's a good kid," said Ed.

"Yeah," said Shane. "She is."

Rather than go to pieces after the attack, Evie and Sarah had insisted on helping with the crisis. The two of them were closer now than ever, and Shane would be there for them both whenever they needed him. A lot of old wounds had finally healed.

"I think this is the house," said Ed, coming to a stop

outside of a house that had once been a small chapel. It still had a stained-glass window in the centre of its triangular frontage, but its spire had been removed. The nameplate on the front door read: *Bella Casa*.

It was a cute little place, with overgrown wildflowers in wrought-iron planters either side of the front doorstep. It was also the kind of place that had a cellar made of stone.

Ed's contact had cleaned up the audio on Vita's video and managed to decipher the roar of the crowd in the final few seconds. People were cheering, but also chanting.

Boing Boing!

It was the triumphant catchphrase of the Baggies – the collective nickname for fans of West Midlands football club West Bromwich Albion. The chanting made it clear Vita had recorded the video within shouting distance of the Hawthorns stadium.

From there, it hadn't taken much. Shane had searched for nearby properties with cellars, basements, etc., while Ed had searched for Italian nationals living in the area. It might have been a difficult task, if not for the fact Ed quickly discovered an old website advertising private language lessons for Italian and Latin. The company was named *Bella Vita*, and the registered business address was right next to the Hawthorns. Operations had wound up eight years ago after the company was dissolved by its only employee – someone named A. Valentino.

Shane was sure they had their man.

"Do we knock?" Ed asked, glancing around at the street. They were on a busy main road with rows of housing on both sides. At the end of the thoroughfare, the

Hawthorns' blue and white Smethwick End rose above the rooftops.

"I suppose we do." Shane rapped on the old wooden door three times.

No one answered.

"Fuck it!" He tried the door handle, a large brass ring. It turned with a resounding *clunk!* and the door swung open on squeaking hinges.

"Hello?" Ed called out. "Mr Valentino?"

"In here."

Shane and Ed shared a look. It was surprising to get such a casual answer, and so quickly. If this was a man responsible for killing a thousand teenagers, wouldn't they be a little more... evasive.

"Um, can we speak to you, please?" Shane yelled, not knowing exactly where to direct his voice. His throat was sore from the swelling. His stitches bulged around his jugular and throbbed constantly.

The hallway was short, with doors to both the left and right. A large wooden cross sat up high on the longest wall facing the entrance.

"You'll have to come through." The voice was firm but unsteady. Mr Valentino sounded like an old man.

Ed moved to the door on the left and wrapped her hand around the door handle. Before she turned it, she looked back over her shoulder at Shane.

Shane nodded. "Go on."

They went into the next room, which was an open-plan space – a living room leading into a tiny sunroom at the back. To the right was a hatch looking into a kitchen. It was a small, stuffy space, and very much lived-in.

The carpets were old-fashioned with a gaudy brown pattern. The wallpaper was peeling in places. All of the furniture was dark wood.

In the corner of the room, an old man sat in a fabric recliner, a blanket across his lap and an oxygen cylinder beside him on a small trolley. As he looked at Ed and Shane, he showed no fear. In fact, he seemed to have been expecting them.

This is Vita?

There was no sofa to sit on, only a pair of wooden-backed chairs around a solid, wooden coffee table. Shane eased his healing body into one, Ed the other. For a moment, Shane just sat there, studying the old man in front of him.

He looks about eighty. Just like Gina said.

Shane decided to get it over with. "Brother Antonio, I've been waiting to have this conversation."

The old man's eyes widened ever so slightly. He reached out and pulled a plastic face mask from a side table and put it to his mouth. After taking in a long suck of oxygen, he straightened up a little in his well-worn chair. With an Italian accent, he said, "It's been a lifetime since anybody called me that."

"You're no longer a monk?"

"Ha!" His skeletal frame rattled with laughter. "They wouldn't have me. I lasted less than three years at the monastery."

Shane sneered. "What was your crime? Fornication with a nun? Mass murder?"

"I attacked the abbot. My temper was a beast of its own back then, but the man deserved it. A vile creature. I have many regrets, but that's not one of them."

"What about Gina D'Amato? Is she a regret?"

A wistful smile crossed the old man's creased face. He had barely a hair on his head, but his dark grey eyebrows were thick and bushy. "One of my greatest. Is she well?"

"She's resting at home with two broken ribs and concussion, thanks to your actions. Why did you send the video to her?"

"I came here for her," he said, his withered hands clenching in his lap. "I came to this rotten country in the hope of finding her. She and I had unfinished business."

"You shunned her. You betrayed her."

He nodded weakly. He was a creature barely alive, rotting where he sat. The entire room smelled stale. "I did, but I thought there would be time to atone. Instead, she fled in the night never to be seen again. Her loss changed me."

Ed cleared her throat. "If you came here to find her, why didn't you?"

"I did. I found her almost immediately. But she had married by then. She was in love. Broken-hearted, I gave up my right to her rather than risk her happiness."

Ed rolled her eyes. "How noble."

"You had no right to her," said Shane. "She didn't even know you'd sent her the video. She thought it was just part of her feed. Had you hoped on a reunion?"

"Yes." A hand went to his mouth as he wheezed. "I hoped that when she saw the ritual, she would know immediately that I was the one behind it. There are very few people in the world who know the words. Most are long dead."

"That's not true," said Ed. "Thanks to you, a lot of people know about the ritual now."

"Why?" said Shane, wanting to leap up and slap this decaying old man in the mouth. Did he even care about what he had done? "Why would you release it onto the Internet? To impress Gina? There has to be a better reason than that."

Antonio's face screwed up. "There's a hundred million reasons for it. I may have left the monastery, but my relationship with God is unbroken. Humanity is sliding into the abyss and it is up to the faithful to do something about it. Our children have become sexual objects, our neighbours have become our enemies. The world is run by false idols and driven by greed. Billionaires hoard wealth while others starve, and deviants target our children. Women drink and vomit in the street. Morals no longer exist, and that awful website, Clip Switch, epitomises it more than anything else."

Ed shook her head and smirked, then raised an eyebrow at Shane. "We were right."

Shane nodded.

"Right about what?" Antonio asked.

"About you. Shane and I were guessing on our way here, about why a person would do this. I think it was Shane who said it was probably just some bitter, religious nutter trying to punish us all for our awful ways."

"It is God's punishment that you all need fear."

Ed tutted. "Who made you the arbiter of our souls? You're just a sad old man, fixated on a woman who moved on with her life. Life has passed you by and you've found yourself alone, sucking on an oxygen tank like some pathetic movie villain. Is this about punishing the wicked, or are you really trying to punish Gina? Did it hurt your feelings when she left without saying goodbye?"

"Are you mocking me? Are you...? Are you...?" He began to hack and cough. He reached out and grabbed his oxygen mask. After several deep inhalations, he got his lungs under control.

"You okay?" asked Shane, unable to be completely heartless.

Antonio nodded. "Lung and thyroid cancer. I'm not long for this world. And I don't even smoke."

"Ironic. Maybe God doesn't approve of your actions."

"I've had lung cancer for several months, young man, and I've lived a devout live. I'm at peace with God's judgement of me."

"Thousands of teenagers and young adults are dead because of you," said Ed, leaning forward in her chair and glaring at the man. "You think God is okay with that?"

"The same God who flooded the earth? Yes, I believe so. The world needed a wake-up call. I have shown them the dangers that await us when we fall to sin and barbarity. Those teenagers were condemned by their own vanity and need for attention."

"Have you seen the news?" Shane sniffed. "They're explaining it a dozen different ways, but no one is claiming it as proof of God."

"And yet, those who were touched directly by Nomon's Ritual know the truth – that there is more than what we see. I have sown the seeds."

"Perhaps," said Shane. "I can see you're an 'ends justify the means' kind of guy, but explain to me what you did exactly. The people who came back... they weren't the same as they were when they were alive."

The old man nodded, and seemed impressed by Shane's assertion. "Nomon's Ritual doesn't truly bring back the dead, not as you might think."

Ed frowned. "What do you mean?"

"You can't pull a soul out of Heaven, nor Hell. Once we pass on, there's no coming back. What the ritual does is summon an imprint, a residue left behind at the moment of a person's death."

"A residue," said Shane. "What's that?"

Antonio took another lungful of oxygen before he answered. "When we pass on to Heaven, we shed our worldly concerns. All of the negative emotions, all of the pains and worries, are left behind. We don't take them with us. In Heaven, only the purest version of us exists. Nomon's Ritual brings forth what's left behind, and what's left contains an imprint of who a person was. You might think of it as their memories made manifest."

"So you can question them about missing artefacts stolen during the war, for example?" said Shane.

Antonio smirked. "Gina told you many tales, I see. The abbot used the ritual to find all kinds of lost treasures, as well as information he could use to gain political power. One of the many reasons I broke both his legs. I still remember the snap like it was yesterday."

"Why do these echoes of the dead want to hurt us? Why do they try to hurt the people they knew in life?"

Antonio shrugged. "I must admit, their violence surprised me. When the monks at the abbey used to perform the ritual, the spirits would often come to us angry

– lost and confused and lacking a soul – but they would also show some semblance of their former selves. Those who were kind in life would manifest the same way when summoned, and yet, time would gradually erode them to madness. For some reason, existing in our realm seems to cause the spirits immense suffering."

"It burns them," said Shane, remembering Millie's grandma. "They think they're doing their loved ones a favour by ending their suffering."

"Perhaps," said Antonio. "But the decay has been happening faster lately. In the past, some spirits would remain calm for many days, the kindest spirits for an entire week. It took time for the suffering to erode whatever goodness remained in them. Something has changed. The darkness has been taking over almost immediately."

"The darkness?"

"Yes. I don't know what it is, but when it used to arrive, the monks would quickly release the spirits. The darkness is a malign force. Something we don't understand."

Shane nodded. "I saw it. It's like black smoke."

"A complete absence of light," said Antonio. "It can suck you right in and tear your soul from your body."

Shane shuddered. He had felt it.

Ed frowned. "So if the ritual didn't work as you expected, does that mean you didn't intend for all those teenagers to die?"

"I didn't wish it, but I was prepared for it. They were necessary sacrifices all the same."

Shane shook his head, horrified to see that this monster could smile and laugh after what he had done. "You need to pay, Antonio. You're a murderer."

"I suppose I am. But before that I was a teacher. Hundreds of pupils have come to me over the decades. Each year, I saw their behaviour worsen. More swearing, more sex, less respect. My last student before I retired was a young man named Daniel Clements. His parents wanted him to learn a language to open up opportunities for him. Instead, I caught him stealing cash from my wallet, and when I confronted him, he beat me. The parents tried to pay me off, but I contacted the police. I trusted in justice." He shook his head, his lips curling. "Daniel spent six months in a youth offender's home and that was it. He came out the same as he went in, a vile, remorseless creature. I didn't know what I was capable of until the next time we met."

Ed groaned. "Capable of what?"

"I tracked Daniel down a few months later and stuck an ice pick in the base of his skull while he walked through an underpass. By ending that boy's life, I did the world a favour. I took a violent animal off the streets. That's when I understood what I needed to be – an instrument of God. Only by decimating today's youth could I pull society out of its tailspin. Their deaths are a warning."

"What you see as sin," said Shane, "others might see as progress. And for every Daniel Clements, there's an Evie Mogg. My niece is a kind, loving kid – and she almost died because of you. Your plan was indiscriminate and evil."

"And it failed," said Ed. "Kids will still have the freedom to be gay, women will still have too much of a good time and puke in the streets, and people will continue to do whatever the fuck they want. It's not perfect, but when was humanity *ever* perfect?"

"Maybe when they used to whip women like Gina bloody and then shun them as whores?" Shane suggested. He looked the old man in the eye, making his disgust clear.

Antonio's face fell, hopefully in shame. "Does she hate me?"

"I don't think Gina hates anyone," said Shane. "She remembers you fondly, if it's any consolation. But unlike you, she is full of love and compassion. She did everything to help the kids you doomed. It put her in hospital."

"I never meant to cause her pain."

"She lived a life of happiness and joy," said Ed. "You really did miss your chance."

Antonio sat for a moment, wheezing. His eyes were yellow as he stared into space. "I'd like you to leave now," he muttered. "I'd like you to..." He started to wheeze and clutched his chest. He reached for his oxygen mask but fumbled it.

Shane hesitated, but then, with a grunt, he grabbed the mask and put it over the man's face. "We're going now, Antonio. We'll leave you to your suffering. Just know that you changed nothing. All you did was spread misery – because you're miserable. You're not righteous; you're just lonely and bitter about a life wasted."

Antonio took several gasps of air and then yanked the mask away. "T-tell Gina that I never forgot her. Tell her that—"

Shane stood up and shook his head. "No. We're not going to tell Gina a thing. She doesn't care about you. Nobody does. Goodbye, Brother Antonio. Prepare to meet the Lord, because your judgement is coming."

Ed got up and joined Shane as they headed out of the

dank living space. Antonio shouted after them angrily before giving in to more wheezing.

Out in the hallway, Shane took a moment, clutching his ribs as he breathed.

"What is it?" Ed asked him.

"Nothing." He went to the end of the hallway and opened the other door, opposite the one they had just come from. Inside was a pair of staircases. One going upwards, the other going down into what looked like a stone cellar.

Ed leant around him and peered down into the darkness. "Guess that's where Vita filmed the ritual."

Shane nodded. It didn't matter now. Antonio had done his damage, but he was finished now. From the looks of him, he'd be dead within the month. This whole thing had been the last dying act of an angry old man. An old man lost and confused in a modern world.

And Shane realised that he had once been heading the same way. When you lived with regret, it froze you in place and allowed life to pass you by.

But I'm looking forward now.

He and Ed stepped outside into the weak sunshine, and they both took a deep breath of fresh air – something Antonio would never again do.

"You okay?" Ed put a hand on his shoulder. "We didn't get many answers. I was hoping for more than just hate and prejudice being the reason behind all this."

He looked at her and smiled. "I got the answers I needed. Mandy's in Heaven. She never left. All that came back was an echo of a terrible, tragic moment."

Ed wrapped an arm around him and propped her head

against his chest. "You think all those teenagers are happy and in Heaven now?"

"I would like to think so. Doesn't make it any easier for the parents who lost them."

"No, it doesn't. So... where to next?"

"Let's go see Gina. She and I still need to get our stories straight about Father Michael. Fortunately, with so many unexplained deaths, the police aren't pushing very hard on anything. If we give them something they can work with, they'll leave it alone."

"Are we too young to retire, Shane?"

"No, we're too poor."

"Yeah, damn it. I could really do with a rest. This has been a really shitty week."

"Least it's over now. Come on, let's head back."

They walked around the corner to a car park outside of a small Co-op. Shane unlocked his brand-new BMW X5 and got in behind the wheel. It didn't feel right, didn't feel comfortable. But a hundred thousand miles on the clock would change that.

He pulled away, the milometer at seventy-four.

CHAPTER 18

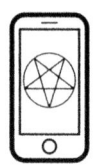

"I'm just running a little late," said Shane to his sister as he stood in his office, holding his mobile phone. "I know, I know. I'm a pain in the arse."

"It's okay," she said. "Just get here when you can. We miss you."

"You saw me yesterday."

"For like five minutes. You're so busy. Take a rest."

"I will soon. Things have just been hectic the last few weeks. Is Evie okay?"

Sarah chuckled. "Mildly disturbed, but her newfound fame and fortune is softening the blow. She has five million followers now."

"And the baby?"

"God, please don't remind me. She's making a pregnancy vlog with Tommy. They think they're a celebrity couple or something. I could tear my hair out."

"It's their world now, we're just living in it."

"Ain't that the truth? I'll put the oven on a little later.

See you when you get here. Oh, and can you pick up Gina? She's still a bit too sore to catch the bus."

"No problem. I'll be with you as soon as I can. Love you."

"Love you too, bro."

Shane ended the call and stood there for a moment, enjoying the contentedness of the moment. His mind was still in knots because of last month's tragic events, yet he felt more hopeful than ever. The first two weeks had been rough, but his shock and trauma had gradually turned to strength and rebirth. It was a chance to reset and be a better man.

Because I couldn't have got any worse.

Bernard had called a six o'clock meeting, which was a bother, but everyone gathered obediently in the conference room. While they waited, Shane stood next to Rachel. To fill the time, he started chatting. They'd been chatting a lot over the last couple of weeks, and he had come to like her a lot. "Hey, um, Rachel, that article you wrote last week about giant squids was great by the way."

She beamed at him. "Thank you so much for letting me write it. My mum was so proud."

"Sure thing." He smiled back, looking her in the eye and holding her gaze. "Listen, I'm sorry I didn't say anything when your dad died a few months back. I'm really sorry."

"That's okay. I didn't expect you to say anything."

"I should have though. You're a nice girl and it's great having you around the office. It sucks that I didn't show you any compassion."

She fidgeted and looked away.

Shane felt awkward too. They had been getting closer recently, but it was still hard to tell what kind of relationship was developing between them.

Shit, should I just do it? Is it weird?
Screw it.

"Hey, um, Rach? I'm having dinner at my sister's tonight. She's cooking a lasagne, nothing special, but do you fancy coming? We can have a few beers maybe, although I'm trying to cut down."

She stared at him for a moment. Signs didn't look good. "Oh, w-would she mind?"

"She would probably be glad to see me interacting with other human beings outside of work, to be honest, and she loves company. You could meet my niece, Evie, as well. Gina will be there too. You remember her, right?"

She gave him a lopsided grin and tucked some of her hair behind one ear. "I would love to come. If it's definitely okay with your sister?"

"It is. We can go straight from here, if that's cool?"

She smiled and nodded. "It's cool."

Bernard walked to the front of the room. He was also beaming. There must have been something in the air today.

"Thanks for staying, everyone," he said. "I just want to start by saying what an awesome week you've all had. Craig, Shane, Rachel, you are all tremendous writers."

Craig blushed. "Oh come on, we know Shane is king around here."

Shane shrugged. "It's true."

Bernard rolled his eyes. "So modest. Yes, your article about Nomon's Ritual last issue went viral and doubled the number of website visitors. Thank you from us all."

Ed, standing in the corner with her camera around her neck, chuckled. "So now we're going bust in six months instead of three?"

"Actually," said Bernard with a knowing smile. "We have enough money now to last another hundred years."

He let that hang there, and everyone glanced around the room in confusion.

"What do you mean?" asked Craig, who was walking on the spot as usual and checking his Fitbit.

"I mean *Splatt!* has a new benefactor. We've been sold."

"To whom?" said Shane. "Who would want to buy a failing bizarro magazine?"

"I would," said a man entering through the door at the side of the room. "Call me a fan of the strange."

Shane almost fell down, which would have been frustrating, seeing as his body had only just started to feel right again. "Evers Nealy?"

The Irish mogul stood at the front of the room with a smug grin on his face. The light glinted on his slick blonde hair. "In the flesh."

Craig started laughing, not just a little, but hysterically. Shane knew it was at his expense. This man was his nemesis. This man was everything that was wrong with the world. Greed and hubris personified.

Shane blinked, wondering if he was dreaming. He noticed then that there was a trio of suited bodyguards out on the main floor. Nealy had entered like a secret agent, appearing from nowhere.

"I understand not everyone will welcome my ownership," Nealy said earnestly, "but you need not fear it. I'll be giving you enough cash to triple your workforce and will fund whatever stories you want to write about. The weirder the better. Bernard will run things as he always has. I will be very hands-off, you have my word."

"Why?" asked Shane, his arms folded. "You've never done a good deed in your life unless there was a profit attached."

Everyone gasped, and Bernard glared, but Shane didn't care. He stared at Nealy, and the man seemed genuinely upset by the remark.

"It's true," he said. "I haven't lived a modest life by any means, and there are many who oppose what I have accomplished. But would you believe me if I told you I'm trying to atone? There are mistakes I need to make up for, and rescuing this little magazine is just one step of many I intend to take towards redeeming my soul."

"No, I wouldn't believe that," said Shane.

Bernard went to speak, but Nealy put a hand up to silence him. "Thought as much. You're Mr Mogg?"

"Correct."

"Mr Mogg, you are the reason I bought *Splatt!*" He chuckled and shook his head. "That name still makes me laugh. Anyway, while all the media were out last month spinning Nomon's Ritual into some kind of terrorist mind control attack or teenage suicide pact, you were the one man who actually published the truth. I read your article about Nomon's Ritual and echoes of the dead, and I believed every word of it."

"You did?" Shane shook his head, trying to think fast, knowing that this man was an intellectual titan, capable of manipulating ninety-nine out of a hundred people in a battle of wits.

Nealy grinned, in a way that was almost infectious. "Would it be possible for you and I to step out for a short moment, Mr Mogg? There's something I would like to discuss."

Bernard nodded at Shane. "He'd be delighted."

"Oh yes I would," said Shane petulantly. He exited the conference room and waited for Nealy to join him. The three suited bodyguards kept close watch.

Like I'm going to do anything?

Nealy took Shane gently by the arm and moved him to one side. "You're right to question my motives, Mr Mogg. Asking questions is your duty, and I want you to continue with that."

"What do you mean?"

"I mean that Nomon's Ritual is just the tip of the iceberg. Do you know that the ritual used to bring back the good and bad parts of people? Dead echoes didn't used to all be bloodthirsty ghouls out for blood. Something has changed. The echoes are all corrupted, only the bad left and the good all but eaten away."

"What are you saying? How do you know about the ritual?"

"I've met the Pope three times, lad. I've known about Nomon's Ritual since I made my first billion. In fact, I even used it myself one time to speak to someone dear to me. What came back then wasn't anything like what has been coming back during the last few weeks. All those dead teenagers..." He shook his head and seemed genuinely pained. "Anyway, all I can tell you is that something has changed. And I mean that on a cosmic level. A darkness is heading our way, and there's going to be many more tragedies to deal with. If possible, I would like to prevent them, and discover what's behind them."

Shane licked his lips and tried to talk. "I... I'm not really following."

"Yes, you are, lad. If the last month hasn't opened your eyes, nothing will. This world of ours is a battleground between the forces of good and evil. Always has been. I fear, however, that the forces of evil are preparing for something big – their very own D-Day. We need to be ready for it. I need to be ready for it."

"But how does that involve me?"

"Isn't that obvious? *Splatt!* is the perfect cover to investigate the strange goings-on in the world. I want you out there, Mr Mogg, doing what you do. Find the anomalies and bring them to my attention. Save lives, like you've just done recently. I know you and your niece are responsible for spreading the cleansing ritual online. Young people are alive today because of you. You're on the right team."

"So you're a general in some upcoming war, is that what you're saying? What does that make me? Cannon fodder?"

Nealy slapped him on the shoulder. "No, my dear boy. You're my recon expert. Special forces. Get in, get out, and then tell me where to send in the troops. We are going to fight back against the darkness and save this world."

Shane shook his head in utter despair. Either this guy was so rich it had made him unstable, or...

Or Nomon's Ritual really is just the tip of the iceberg and there's more to life than what we all thought. How much is there that people don't see? Last month I didn't believe in ghosts. Now I know for sure that they exist. Is there more?

Vampires, werewolves, demons?

"How do you know all this?" Shane asked. "How do you know something's coming?"

Nealy smiled. "Ever heard of the cursed manuscripts?"

"No."

"Well, I have them. I have them all."

"You've lost me."

Nealy patted him on the shoulder again. "No, Mr Mogg, I have found you. It's time to get to work. Are you in?"

He shook his head and blinked slowly. "Um... yes?"

"That's what I like to hear."

Shane stood staring into space for several minutes, while Nealy got to know his colleagues in the conference room. He felt like he was dreaming. Something big had just happened – something monumental – but he still didn't really know what.

Eventually, Rachel found him and broke him out of his daze. "You ready to go have dinner?" she asked him. "Or do you want to stay and schmooze with one of the richest men in the world who is now our boss?"

He blinked several times and then shuddered. "Y-yeah, I'm ready to go to dinner. Are you?"

She nodded. "Everything okay?"

"Nowhere close to okay," he said. "But that's a worry for tomorrow." He linked arms with Rachel, and it immediately felt right. His worries went away. "Let's go eat."

On their way out, Shane grabbed Ed and invited her to dinner too. She and Sarah had hit it off lately, and they were quickly becoming friends.

"Did you hear the news?" Ed asked him as they

headed out to his car. "Nealy just doubled everyone's pay and took me back on full time. No more curtains and quilts for me."

Shane pulled a face. "I hope that doesn't mean you plan on moving out?"

"Depends," she said.

"On what?" asked Rachel, smiling.

"On whether or not I can turn Shane's sister."

Shane gasped. "Don't you dare!" Then he reconsidered. "Actually, go right ahead. She could do a lot worse than you, Ed."

She linked his other arm. "Ah, look at you. You're like a whole, well-rounded person now."

He opened his car door and a load of empty McDonald's cartons fell out onto the floor.

Ed groaned. "Well, almost."

"I'm working on it," he said. "One bad habit at a time."

Rachel picked up the cartons and smirked at Ed while she knelt. "You and I can whip him into shape, huh? There's a man in there somewhere."

"There is," said Shane. "I'm looking forward to you all finally meeting him."

They got inside the car, and Shane started the engine.

"Oh," said Ed. "Why did Nealy pull you aside, by the way?"

He looked at her for a moment. "If I had to tell you some really messed-up shit, would you want me to tell you tonight, or in the morning?"

She thought about it. "In the morning. Let's not ruin dinner."

"Good call," he said. "Just be prepared for me to ruin

CHAPTER 18

breakfast, because I've got some stuff to tell. Nealy's expanding his business. He wants to save the world."

From the forces of darkness.

"That's good, right?"

Shane nodded. "Yeah, except the problem with most billionaires is that whenever they try to save the world, they end up making it worse."

"Worse than this?" said Ed. "Surely things are bad enough already."

Shane pulled out of the car park. "One thing I've learned is that things can always get worse. Always."

Rachel put a hand on his knee. "They can get better too."

He nodded, smiled, and then nodded again. "Yeah, you're right. Sometimes things get better. Let's hope for the best."

But expect the worse.

Shane pulled onto the main road, to go eat lasagne with his friends and family, and to be grateful that, for tonight at least, life was good.

UPLOADING...
    UPLOADING...
    UPLOAD COMPLETE.
    VIDEO NAME: NoMoN'S RTL 2.0
    VIDEO UPLOADER: VITA.NEW
    VISIBILITY: PUBLIC

PUBLISH NOW?

YES.

WANT FREE BOOKS?

Don't miss out on your FREE Iain Rob Wright horror pack. Five terrifying books sent straight to your inbox.

No strings attached & signing up is a doddle.

Just Visit IainRobWright.com

ALSO BY IAIN ROB WRIGHT

Animal Kingdom
AZ of Horror
2389
Holes in the Ground (with J.A.Konrath)
Sam
ASBO
The Final Winter
The Housemates
Sea Sick, Ravage, Savage
The Picture Frame
Wings of Sorrow
Hell on Earth (6 books)
TAR
House Beneath the Bridge
The Peeling
Blood on the bar
Escape!
Dark Ride
12 Steps
The Room Upstairs
Soft Target, Hot Zone, End Play, Terminal
The Spread (6 books)
Witch
Zombie
Hell Train
Maniac Menagerie

Iain Rob Wright is one of the UK's most successful horror and suspense writers, with novels including the critically acclaimed, THE FINAL WINTER; the disturbing bestseller, ASBO; and the wicked screamfest, THE HOUSEMATES.

His work is currently being adapted for graphic novels, audio books, and foreign audiences. He is an active member of the Horror Writer Association and a massive animal lover.

www.iainrobwright.com
FEAR ON EVERY PAGE

For more information
www.iainrobwright.com
author@iainrobwright.com

Copyright © 2022 by Iain Rob Wright

Cover Photographs © Shutterstock

Artwork by Carl Graves at Extended Imagery

Editing by Richard Sheehan

All rights reserved.

No part of this book may be reproduced in any form or by any electronic or mechanical means, including information storage and retrieval systems, without written permission from the author, except for the use of brief quotations in a book review.

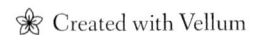

❋ Created with Vellum

Printed in Great Britain
by Amazon